Brite and Fair

Henry A. Shute

BRITE and FAIR

BY HENRY A. SHUTE
Author of "The Real Diary of a Real Boy"

1920

BRITE AND FAIR

June 2th, 186—-sunday nite. i have been to chirch and sunday school today, not to the unitarial. we are going to the congrigasional now becaus Keene and Cele are singing in the quire. so we go there. i had ruther go to the unitarial becaus Beany and Pewt go there. Beany blows the organ and sumtimes he peeks out behine the organ and maiks a feerful face and maiks everybody laff. once Beany he thummed his nose to old Chipper Burly. Chipper he was the sunday school supperintendent and was beeting time for the scholers to sing and Chipper he tirned round quick and see Beany, and Chipper he jest hipered into the organ log and grabed Beany by the coler and yanked him out of the lof and wauked him out of the chirch. then he got Micky Goold to blow the organ and Beany he lost his gob for 2 sundays, but Micky went to sleep 2 or 3 times and snoared feerful and they had to waik him up and once he hollered rite out loud. so Mickey he lost his gob and they got Beany back. They tride Pewt and then Game Ey Watson, Beanys brother but they was wirse than Micky. so they hired Beany. he is the best and only lets the wind out one or two times every sunday and the organ sounds like a goos but that aint so bad as going to sleep and hollering goldarn it lemme alone is it?

we had a new minister today, miser Larned has gone away for all summer. the new minister preeched about not killing flise and buggs and wirms and bumbelbeas and yeller jacket hornits. he sed they had a rite to live jest as mutch as peeple and we hadent augt to kill them. i spose it is all rite to let a muskeeter or flee or one of them 3 cornered flise that hangs round a swimmin hole bite you terrible and not even yip. how about bedbugs.

June 3, 186—-today is washing day and i had to lug about a million pales of water for old mis Dire, Sams mother whitch comes over mondays. her hands is all sriveled up they has been in hot water so mutch. mother she sed that was the reason when i asted her and father he laffed and sed he had been in hot water all his life and he wasent sriveled a bit. mother she laffed two. father aint sriveled for he weigs 214 lbs. i gess he dident meen that kind of hot water eether. i am tired most to deth tonite.

June 4, 186—-brite and fair. i went fishing today with Potter Goram in the morning and was going again in the afternoon but i dident get home in time to help them flap flise out of the dining room and mother woodent let me go to pay me for being lait. darn it. every day we have to flap flise out of the dining room. we all grab our flapers and begin to flap from one end of the room to the other flaping them into the kitchen. then we shet the doors and keep them out. it is fun flaping for most always i can give Keene a good bat in the ear with a flaper when she aint looking. then she gives me one on the snoot and then we jest go at it til mother stops us. she maiks us take tirns now. ferst it is me and Cele and then it is Cele and Keene. it is never me and Keen any more. mother says we fite enuf without fiting when there is china and crockery and glass round and things to eat two. ennyway it is tuf on Cele to have to do it all the time becaus she is good and dont fite.

i told mother what old mister minister sed and mother she sed that if old mister minister had to fite flise for every mossel of food he et she gessed he woodent say mutch about not killing them. Aunt Sarah she sed so two. flise is wirse this summer. we have got a new set of fli screnes. little ones for the butter plates, bigger ones for the sass plates and some grate big ones for the meat plates and the cake basket. we had to get them becaus the old ones was woar out and i took the big one and kept a young robin in nearly a week and mother maid me let him go and never wood use the screne again. we tride to have muzlin screnes to the wiinders but the cat and the dog jumped through them if the doors was shet. mother says she dont know what she will do if the flise get enny wirse.

June 5, 186—-it raned last nite. brite and fair today. it raned hard and the sidewalks was filed with pudles of water. me and Beany had lots of fun spatering peeple. the way we do it is this. when we see sum peeple waulking on the sidewaulks we run by them fast and stamp hard in the pudles and the water spaters all over them. we dont do it to wimmen and girls. but we do to men and fellers. it is lots of fun to hear them sware. Beany got 2 bats in the ear and a kick and i got 3 bats in the ear and 2 kicks. so i beat Beany. one of the kicks was a peeler. ennyway we had lots of fun.

today all the fellers and girls got a letter from old mister minister and it had in it a peace of poetry like this

do you know how menny flise fli about in the warm sun
how menny fishes in the water
god has counted eevry one

every one he called by naim
when into the wirld it caime.

there was a lot moar to it but i aint got no time to wright enny moar
of such stuf as that. i showed it to mother and she said when he got
older peraps he wood know moar.

June 6, 186—-clowdy today. jest the day to go fishing but i had to ho
in the garden. if it had raned i coodent ho the beans becaus if you ho
when it is wet they will be all covered with black specks like
Whacker Chadwick had when he had the measles. i have et them
like that and they taist jest like those yeller spots in creem tarter
bisquit when it gets way in a corner of your mouth up under your
ear on the inside and you cant reech it with a drink of water.
ennyway it dident rane and i had to ho whitch is jest my luck.
mother let me go at 4 oh clock to go in swimming with the
Chadwicks and Potter and Skinny Bruce. we had sum fun tying
gnots in Skinnys shert sleev. we bet Skinny coodent swim across
under water and while he was doing it we wet his shert sleves and
tide hard gnots in them. Skinny coodent unty them becaus he aint
got enny front teeth. most of the fellers can unty gnots eesy with
their teeth but Skinny had to go home with his shert tide around his
neck and his jacket buttened up tite.

the 3 cornered flise has come and bit Skinny terrible while he was
trying to get into his shert. i hollered oh Skinny, do you know how
meny flise fli about in the warm sun and Skinny he up and chased
me as far as Gilmans barn and wood have chased me further but he
hadent enny shert on. i guess if the old minister had heard Skinny
sware he woodent have sed mutch more about flise.

June 7, 186—-brite and fair. not mutch today. tonite the band played
in the band room. Ed Tilton has got a new basehorn. it is auful shiny
and almost as long as he is. Potsy Dirgin played a fife. father says
peraps i can have a fife some day but a cornet costs two much
money. they played a new march and a peace that mother said was a
romanse from leeclare. mother used to play it. i asked her where
leeclare was and she sed it was a mans name. Cele can hear a band
peace once and play it on the piano jest as good as they can. i can
whistle it all rite but she can put in the alto and the treble and the
base jest like it is rote.

June 8, 186—-brite and fair. not mutch today only swiming and playing base ball and a fite down town whitch old Swain and old Kize the poliseman stoped. tonite we all have to take a bath in the tub in the kichen. Mother maiks me use soft sope. the others use casteel sope but mother says soft sope is the only thing that will get me cleen. it stings terrible when it gets into a cut or a soar place. after a feler has been stang with soft sope in a cut on his hand or on his leg with a nail or a peace of glass or a tin can he dont care mutch for anything but a yeller jakit hornit. i had to lug all the water for the tub and i had to fill it with fresh water for every one of us. they aint enny sense in that. onct wood have been enuf. twict wood ennyway.

June 9, 186—-Sunday again brite and fair it is always brite and fair sundays so fellers has to go to chirch. last nite when Keene was going to bed we heard sum feerful screaches in her room. mother and aunt Sarah just hipered upstairs thinking Keene had tiped over the lamp and was burning to deth and both hollering for mecy sakes what is the matter. nothing was the matter only a dorbugg had flew into her hair and stuck there and scart her most to deth. mother said she had augt to be ashaimed of herself. mother give me the dorbugg and i am going to put it down Beanys back. i bet Beany will gump.

Beany come to our chirch today. they wasnt eny chirch at the unitarial. in sunday school Beany spoke a peace about a fli. it said god made the little fli but if you crush it it will die and then he set down. the rest of us laffed but the minister told us it was the best peace of all and it showed that Elbridge, that is Beany you know, was kind to flise and insex of all kinds and if we was all like Elbridge, Beany you know, the wirld woodent have as mutch mizzery in it. we was all mad with Beany for showing off and we were going to lam him one after school let out. he cought a big bumbelbea whitch had flew in to the window and took sum wax and hitched a long white thread to the bumbelbea and let him go and he flew all over the chirch with that long white thread hanging down like a kite tail. everybody laffed and the girls screemed and ducked there heads down and the minister tride a long while to ketch the bumblelbea and finely he cought it by the thred and it clim up the thred and stang him and he sed drat the pesky thing and snaped his fingers and the bea flew out of the window. then the minister sed it was natural for the bea to be scart only he sed terrorfide whitch meens the saim, and it dident know who was befrending it. but it was crool to tie a string to him and the boy whitch done it wood suffer. enny way he sed you woodent do it wood you Elbridge and

4

Beany he sed no sir. then Beany he went behine the organ and we sung oh how happy are we all in our little sunday school and Beany let the wind out of the organ 2 times. so we aint going to lam Beany. ennyway the ministers thum is all swole up.

June 10, 186—-i put the dorbugg down Beanys back. you aught to heard him holler.

June 11, 186—-rany and cold. a big black ant has got 2 nippers and can bite like time. i am going to put one down Beanys back some day.

June 11, 186—-the cat drank sum fli poison today and dide. we are going to have some fli paper after this. father says all you got to do is to get sum pich and spred it on brown paper and the flise will get their hine legs all stuck up on it and die. so tomorrow i am going down to the sawmill and scraip a lot of pich off the ends of the logs.

June 12, 186—-brite and fair. today i scraiped a lot of pich off the logs and then took it home and tonite father warmed it until it was all runny and spred it on a lot of sheets of brown linen. it was awful sticky, i bet it wood hold a cat, then befoar we went to bed he put 1 in the kitchen sink and 2 on the table and 2 on the dining room table and 2 in the setting room, and he hung one up over the sink to kech flise on the wall. well in the middle of the nite i heard awful swareing down stairs and heard father hollering for mother to come down. i set up and lissened. i gnew it wasent berglers for father cood nock the stuffing out of enny bergler and if it was i gnew he woodent let mother come down where they was dainger. so i lissened and oh time how father was swareing. i never heard enny such swareing in my life, and father aint a swareing man.

then i heard mother begin to laff. then i gnew it was all right. so i lissened. then i heard father say for god's sake get the sizzers and cut this damn linen off my head, and mother sed keep still and stop swareing, and father he sed, i have got to keep still for i am all stuck up and i had augt to be aloud to sware. then he laffed. then mother she said i am afrade i shall have to cut off most of your hair, and father he sed get hold of the end of it and yank quick. then i heard him say why dont you pull a poor cusses head off and she sed i gess i have jugging by the looks of this linen. it is all covered with hair. then i heard her cutting with sizzers and then he sed it is lucky i came down in my shert tale if i had been dressed i wood have had to go to bed tomorrow until you went down town to by me a new sute. you see father had gone down for a drink of water in the dark and had got into the fli paper. father had augt to know better than to do that becaus once he drunk sum water out of a dipper in the pale in the dark and the nex morning he found my squirrel drowneded in the pale and he never gnew whether it was drownded before he drank or after he drunk and it made him sick to wonder whitch was whitch. well after a while father and mother come up stairs again, i cood hear Keene and Cele gigling in there room and i wanted to holler do you know how many flise fli about in the warm sun but i dident dass to. this morning mother sed that father he sed he forgot all about the drink of water and dident get it but we aint going to have enny more fli paper round the house. it was wirse than having a poliseman with handcufs and twisters.

June 13, 186—-i am having awful tuf luck with my hens this year. Miss Dires cat cougt 8 of my chickings this week. i went over to tell her about it and have her pay for the chickings and she sed how did i know it was her cat and i sed it was a old yeller cat that she had for 2 or 3 years and i see it runing with a chicking in its mouth. then she sed it wasent her cat and i sed all right i am going to kill it with a rock and she sed you better not kill it if you know what is good for you and i sed what do you care if it aint your cat and she sed i will maik it mine if you kill it and you will wish you was ded if you kill it. so i went home. then Nellie steped on my best hen whitch was scraching behine her in the stall and squashed her almost as flat as a doremat. enny way i have got to do sumthing about that cat. i wonder what old mister minister wood do if a cat killed his chickings. i supose he wood say it is rong to kill a cat and that a cat had as mutch rite to live as—-as—-well as old Mis Dire.

June 14, 186—-2 chickings gone today. i let a rock ding at the cat and jest missed her. i wish i had a bull dog.

June 15, 186—-went in swiming today. 3 times. The 3 cornered flise are auful and bit like time. i squashed lots of them and they wont fli about in the warm sun enny more. I dont cair. me and Pewt are going to set a trap for the cat. Pewt can make bully box traps. if he ketches the cat i am going to give him my collexion of birds egs. it is werth it. i aint got menny chickings left.

June 16, 186—-brite and fair of course. it always is sunday. i went to chirch sunday and to sunday school. i wanted to go to the Unitarial but father he sed no i wood go where he told me to or i coodent go at all. i thought i had got him there and i sed all rite i will stay to home and he sed all rite you can stay to home and stay in bed. so i thougt i had better go to chirch and i sed all rite i will go to chirch. i told him as long as we had got a phew in both chirches someone augt to set in it once in a while. the minister is going to get up a club to study insex throug the telescope and to lern us about their ways. he said beas have queans and droans and aunts have a government and keeps cows. i wonder if he xpects us to beleeve that. and flees can be traned to ride a vellosipede but he dident know that if you ketch a big grashoper and say grashoper gashoper gray give me sum molasses and then fli away the grashoper will give you some molasses. just think he dident know that and he dident know that ef you squashed a caterpiller it would rane before nite. we have all got to join the club. i wish i had staid in bed.

tonite Pewt come over with a big box trap and we set it in the hen coop and left the dore open. i bet we will ketch her. we bated it with a peace of pikerel.

June 17, 186—-Gosh what do you think. we have caugt that cat. this morning i went to the hencoop and the trap was sprung. when i shook it a little i cood hear the old cat growl and spitt. so i nailed the cover down so he coodent get out and gess what we done with him. tonite after dark we carried the box to the deepo and put him on the nite fraight trane for Haverhill. nobody see us. we wated till the trane started and then went home. Pewt wanted to drownd the old cat but i thougt if we did i wood have to lie about it and while i can lie good if i have to i had ruther not. and it wood be eesier to say i dident know ehere the cat was peraps it wood be in Haverhill and peraps in Boston.

June 18, 186—-brite and fair. Gosh what do you think. the first thing i see this morning was that old cat setting on Mis Dires steps. i thougt she must have comeway back from Haverhill but after breckfast old mother Moulton come over and asted me if i had seen her cat. she was terrible xcited and asted me more than 40 questions but i dident know ennything. Pewt come down and sed she had been to his house and to Beanys and all over the naborhood. gosh i bet we caugt her cat and sent it away. ennyway what rite had her old cat in my hencoop.

tonite me and Pewt set a new trap and bated it with a fresh sucker. i have got to get the old yeller cat. one more chickling disapeared to day.

June 19, 186—-it raned hard last nite. i gess cats staid to home and dident go out. this morning the trap wasent spring. had to ho in the garden after it dride up. toniet we put a big shiner in the trap for bate.

June 20, 186—-we cogt that old cat today. i know it was her this time becaus when the cover come down it pinched her tale and there was a bunch of yeller hair in front of the trap. tonite we put the trap on the fraight trane and that is the last of that old cat. old mother Moulton is still hunting for her cat. i wonder if the 2 cats will know eech other when they meet in Haverhill. i xpect mis Dire will be over tomorrow to find out where her old cat is. i dont know where she is. i havent hit her or killed her and i dont know what has become of her.

June 21, 186—-brite and fair. today i saw that old cat again. i wonder whose cat we cought. i had to pay Pewt 10 cents for his traps. we set another for tonite.

June 22, 186—-awful hot today. i dident ketch that cat. i went fishing today for some cat bate. went in swimming 5 times. got some good shiners. i have found out whose cat we sent to Haverhill the last time. there was a peace in the Exeter News-Letter whitch sed. lost a valuble black and yeller striped tiger cat. a grate pet. had on a red satin bow. a suteable reward will be paid for infirmation as to whareabouts. A. P. Blake. gosh A. P. Blake is Mager Blake who owns the Squamscot Hotel. I know that cat. i wish me and Pewt gnew some peeple in Haverhill peraps we cood get the reward. tonite i paid Pewt another ten cents and we set another trap. i wonder whose cat we will get nex time.

June 23, 186—-brite and fair, i never knew it to rane sunday. cougt another, dont know whose cat it is. if we open the cover the cat will gump out and if we dont sum body elces cat may get sent Haverhill. ennyway enny cat whitch is cougt in my hencoop has got to take chances.

tonite we sent it away on the trane. we almost got cougt putting it on. went to chirch and sunday school. Beany has got his gob back at the unitarial and has went back there, so there wasent enny fun. i heard old Mis Dire calling her cat tonite for most an hour. i guess we got that old cat at last.

June 24, 186—-Mis Dire was calling her cat this morning. she come and did the washing today but she dident say ennything about her cat but i think she was uneezy and she looked at me sort of hard. i bet she thinks i have killed her cat.

June 25, 186— today old Mis Dire come over. i was in the shed and i saw her go waulking stiflegged. after a minit or too mother called me. i pertended i dident hear her and kept on spliting wood, then she come out and told me old Mis Dire sed i killed her cat and wanted to ast me some questions and mother sed now if you have killed her cat tell the truth. i sed i anit killed it or hit it or drowneded it and i dont know where it is. so we went in. old Mis Dire was there mad as time and she sed now Harry Shute i want to know what you have did with my cat and if you lie to me, then mother sed quick ome moment Misses Dire if you are going to ast him enny questions you have got to do it in a different way if you xpect enny anser. mother she looked at old Mis Dire and old Mis Dire looked at mother mad as time but mother had a kind of funny look in her eyes not a mad look but a kind of look that made old Mis Dire back water pretty quick. then old Mis Dire sed you throwed a rock at my cat last week and i sed yes i did and i wish i had hit hir and killed her but i dident. then she said you and that misable Watson boy and that jalebird of a Purinton boy have drowned my cat and i sed i dont know about them but i dont beleve they done it becaus they dident have enny chickings but hope to die and cross my throte i havent seen your cat or hit your cat or drowned your cat and i dont know where she is i honest dont. old Mis Dire asted me more than 40 questions and after a while she went home. she was pretty grumpy and sed sumbody had got to pay for her cat but i guess she desided i dident know ennything about it. she went over to Pewts and to Beanys but dident find out ennything.

Mother she was glad i told the truth and i did dident i? i dident hit her old cat, or killed it or drowned it or see it and i dont know where it is. mother told father about it when he come home from Boston and father sed dam her old cat. i wont have you bothered about her old cat. i wood have told her to go to the devel. mother laffed and sed no you woodent George you wood have felt bad and pitted her as i did. she is a poar old woman and it is two bad for ennyone to kill her pet cat. ennyway that is over and i aint got to wurry over my chickings enny more. i wish i dassed tell father about it but i am afraid father wood tell mother for a goke and if mother dident think it was rite she wood make me go to Haverhill or Boston and hunt for them 3 old cats. father i know wood laff his head off but i dassent tell him. 3 old cats sounds like a base ball game dont it. ennyway me and Pewt made 3 home runs dident we.

June 26, rany. dident do ennything today.

June 27, 186—-i havent wrote ennything about school becaus i dident like school and dident like to think about it. the fellers is all rite and we have sum fun playing base ball and foot ball and corram and duck on a rock and nigger baby. but we have to study like time and they aint hardly enny fites becaus if 2 fellers has a fite old Francis licks time out of them and recess aint very interestin if they aint enny fites. school closes tomorrow and i am so glad i dont know what to do. i gess old Francis wanted to celibrait today for he licked 9 fellers. Skipy Moses for paisting Medo Thirsten in the eye with a spit ball and Chitter Robinson for not singing in tune and he cant if he wanted to so what is the sence of licking him i dont see and Pewt for putting a carpit tack in Pheby Taylors seat. Pheby he is a feller you know and when he set on it he gumped up lively and let out a yell. Pheby dident tell he aint that kind of a feller but old Francis seamed to know it was Pewt and snached him bald headed in two minits and Whacker Chadwick for wrighting a note to a girl and Pozzy Chadwick for maiking up a face at him when he was licking Whack and Bug Chadwick for telling him to stop when he was licking Pozzy. the Chadwicks all got licked the same day. it aint the ferst time eether by a long chork and Skinny Bruce for drawing sumthing on the school house fence that hadent aught to be drew and Pacer Gooch for calling Gran Miller a nigger and he is a nigger whitch dont seem rite to me and Human Nudd, his name is Harman but we call him Human for wrighting with a squeaky slate pensil. he hadent enny other. i gess old Francis gnew this was his last day for licking for he never licks on Xibition day but is as nice as pye.

June 28, 186—-Gosh school is over. i cant hardly beleeve it. lots of peeple come in today and of course all the good boys and girls spoke peaces and direlogs and done xamples on the blackboard. Huh i am glad i am not a good scholar and a faveret of the teecher. last of all we give old Francis a silver pensil on a chane. the wirst of it was i had to chip in ten cents. the Chadwicks give a dollar. Whack sed that if he had gnew that they were all 3 going to be licked yesterday they wood have spent the dollar and woodent have given nothing. they needed that dollar two. ennyway school is out till September hurray.

June 29st. i just took it eezy to-day. the ferst day of vacation always seams to me like when you find a five cent peace in a pair of your last years britches. you can spend it for ennything you want and you havent got to save it or put it in your bank or by sumthing that you need. so yesterday after school closed i split up wood enuf for today and sunday, and today i just dident do nothing. a man and 2 wimen hired my boat and wanted me to row them up river but i told them i had a weak arm.

one of the wimen said poar boy what is the matter with it and i sed it dident know but it trubles me a good deal. then the other one sed whitch arm is it and i sed the right one and she sed you must be lefthanded and i sed yes i am a little. i lied about that but i dident lie about my week arm or about my truble with it. both my arms is week. if they wasent i cood lick Pewt and it trubles me becaus my arms is so skinny. the fellers laff at my legs two.

well the man hired my boat and i went with them and the man rew all the way and i had a good time only i had to be cairful to keep my right hand in my jacket pocket most of the time and point out things to them with my left hand. ennyway i cood row with one hand better than that man cood with too. he splashed and cougt crabs and once his heels went up and he went rite over on his back the wimen laffed and he laffed two.

June 30, 186—-brite and fair. i gnew it wood be. we had a new minister today. old mister minister preeched sumwhere elce but he come back in the afternoon to sunday school and started his club. everybody had to join. most of the fellers dident want to. Chick Chickering says he is glad he dont go to our chirch becaus if he did he coodent colect enny more butterflise and kill them with ether and stick them in a box with a pin. Chicks father is a minister two and he goes fishing and birdseging and butterfliing with Chick. i am glad my father isent a minster but if he was i wood want him to be like Chick Chickerings father. Gosh i always laff when i think of father being a minister.

he woodent be getting up clubs to save the lifes of flise and snaiks and intch wirms and moth millers and cockroches, but he wood gnock enny feller pizzle end upwards that raised time in chirch. today we had to a sine a book and pay five cents and promise not to take the life of animal or bird or reptil or insex.

Pop Clark asked what a feller had augt to do if a mad dog come down the street fomeing at the mouth and biting and taring rite and lef, or if a poizen adder or ratlesnaik coiled round your hine leg. the minister sed if it caim to be a question of the life of a human being or of an animal or a reptil of coarse the life of a human being shood be spaired. so he has got sum sence but not mutch.

June 31, 186—-i ment July 1, brite and fair. hoap it wont rane on the 4th. jest as soon as vacation comes i have a lot of gobs to do. spliting wood and going errands and cleening out the cellers and the barn and wirking in the garden. i woder what peeple think a vacation is for. i try to do evrything mother wants becaus in 3 days it will be the 4th.

July 2, 186—-only 1 day after this before the 4th. i went up to Pewts today. he has borowed Harris Cobbs cannon. it is an old lunker. Pewt says if you put in six fingers of powder and wads and then fill it to the muzle with grass and ram it tite it will shaik the winders all over town.

July 3, 186—-tomorrow is the 4th. i am going to get up at 3 oh clock. father says that is the erliest and if i get up one minit before that i wont go out at all. it seams to me 3 oh clock is pretty lait. sum of the fellers stay out all nite.

July 5. brite and fair. i was so tired last nite that i coodent wright. i dident go to bed until nearly leven and i got up at 3 oh clock. it was the best 4th i ever had. Pewt's cannon xploded the ferst time. we loded it to the muzle and put the muzle rite agenst the stone step of old Nat Weeks house. then we lit the fusee and run. i gess it is lucky we done it for there was a feerful bang and a big flash jest like when litening strikes a tree rite in front of your house and a big hunk of that cannon went rite throug old Bill Greenleafs parlor winder and took sash and all and gnocked a glass ship in a gloab that the glassblewers blowed into forty million peaces and gnocked a big hunk out of the marbel top table and sent the things on the whatnot all over the room.

Bill he come downstairs in his shert tale and hollered and swore so you cood hear him fer eigt miles eesy. me and Pewt and Beany hid behine Pewts fathers paint shop and lissened. Nat Weeks he come out and old printer Smith and old Bill Morrill. Old Ike Shute dident. i gess he dident dass to. we cood hear them talking it over and cood hear Bill holler and sware and Bills wife say mersy sakes aint this dredful. they thogt it must have been did by Flunk Ham and Chick Randall or the Warren boys, all big fellers becaus they sed it must be big fellers to have sutch a big cannon. so me and Pewt and Beany clim over Fifields back fence and went down town throug Spring street.

Beany set fire to a bunch of fire crackers in his poket and birnt him so he can only sit down on one side. Fatty Melcher stumped Pewt to hold a firecracker in his mouth and let it go off. it is eezy enuf. all you have got to do is to put the end between your teeth and lite the other end and shet your eys. it will go off and burst in the middle and all you will get is a few sparks that dont hurt mutch. but this one was a flusher and it flushed at the end whitch was in Pewts mouth and a stream of sparks went rite down Pewts gozzle. you would have dide to see Pewt spitt and holler and drink water. he drank most a gallon and he wont speak to me becaus laffed.

All the Chadwicks got birned when they was blowing up old Buzell's fence posts, they was lots of fites down town and a house on Franklin Street and a barn on Stratam road birned up. it was the best 4th i ever gnew. Father sed about 2 more 4ths and he wood go out of bisiness.

i sed 2 4ths is eigt and he sed dont you try to be funny. if you do you will get a bat in the ear. so i shet up. when father says that it is about time to shet up.

July 6, brite and fair. saterday again. it is funny when i am in school i am crasy for it to be saterday but when it is vacation i hate to have saterday come. it means 2 things that aint very good. one is that another weak of vacation has gone and the other is that the next day is sunday both of whitch is prety tuf. tonite me and father went in swimming at the gravil. we had a good swim and then we floted down river. it was warm and the treetoads was crokeing and a peewee was peeweeing high up in a elm tree and bats was fliing and it was fine. evry now and then a fish wood splash or a mushrat dive.

when we got home all the folks was setting on the front steps and we got talking about the doodlebug club. father he calls it that. father sed they aint no fool like a dam fool and sed that once when he was in school his teecher old Ellis the father of Rody Ellis that i went to school to used to paist time out of the fellers jest for nothing. so the fellers they got prety sick of it and one day Jim Melcher and of coarse father, he and Jim Melcher always went together and Charles Taylor two and Oliver Lane and 2 or 3 others went out and batted down about a pint of bumblebeas with shingles. they got stang 2 or 3 times a peace but no feller minds being stang in a good caus. so the next day they went to school erly and poured all them ded beas in his old lether seat.

well old Ellis come in and rung the bell and sed prair and paisted time out of 2 or 3 fellers for exercise and toar the sherts off 2 or 3 others for old acquantence saik so father sed and then he set down hard in his chair and more than forty of the stings of them ded bumblebeas riggid in deth so father sed ran rite into him. well he let out a yell you cood have heard at Hampton Beach and gumped

rite over his desk and run out of the school house howling and holding hisself in both hands and sweling up feerful in grate aggony. and father he sed he was stang in forty seven places and swole up so that they had to get old killpigger Haley i mean pig killer Haley to get his briches off with a skining knife.

i wonder if old mister minister wood like bumblebeas if we done that to him.

July 7, rany as time. i thought i woodent have to go to chirch but what do you think it cleered up and the sun come out a hour before chirch. how is that for tuf luck.

July 8, rany not hard but drissly. i wood have went fishing today but there was a thunder shower this morning and fish wont bite after thunder but go down in deep holes and lay still. this afternoon we had the meating of the club. the minister talked lots and ansered questions. i asted him if we had aught to tare down spiders webs becaus they kiled flise. he sed yes then i asted him if the spider woodent starve to deth if he coodent ketch flise. then he sed spiders was sumtimes poizinus and i asted him if he had ever been bit by a horsefli. then we had speeking and Beany spoke his peace about

    god made the little fli
    but if you crush it it will die

and then my sister Cele spoke the peace

> do you know how meeny flise
> fli about in the warm sun

and the minister clapt his hands and we all did two.

then Tomtit Thompson sed he had a new peace about insex and the minister asted him to speak it and Tomtit dident want to, but the minister sed he had aught to be willing to help out in a good caus. Tomtit he sed he was afrade the minister woodent like it but the minister sed he was very sure he wood like it and so Tomtit he stood up and made a bow and sed his peace and it was jest bully.

> now i lay me down to sleep
> while the bedbugs round me creap
> if one should bite before i waik
> i hope to god his jaw will braik

and what do you think the minister he got mad and told Tommy he was a bran from the birning and a apostate. i thought they wasent but 12 apostates ever and wasent enny now but that is what he called Tommy and he throwed him out of the club by the ear, wisht it had been me.

Well after Tommy had went the minister talked to us about how wicked it was for Tommy to use the name of god in sutch a conexion. I asted him why it was wicked to use it in conexion with a bedbugg when it wasent wicked to use it in conexion with a fli like Beanys peace and my sister Celes and he sed one was used in the spirrit of love and the other in the spirrit of hate. then we sung a hynm and went home. i wish i was Tomtit Thompson.

July 9, 186—-brite and fair. gosh what do you think. the committy of the chirch came to our house today and asted mother if she wood have the minister to supper as it was her tirn. mother sed certenly i wood be very glad to entertain him. after the committee left i sed gosh mother you told a awful whacker to them old wimmen when you sed you wood be glad to do it dident you. mother she laffed and sed peraps it woodent be as deliteful as it mite be but she wood try hard to be glad to do it and if i wood do my part and all the rest wood we cood give him a good supper and it woodent hurt us to do it. so we have all got to duff in.

July 10, it is going to be a weak from Friday nite that the minister is coming. Friday nite is the nite they have prair meeting and he will have to go prety soon after supper so he wont be there very long. aunt Sarah she sed what if he invites us to go and mother she sed she gessed father wood have a pretty good xcuse ready. she never gnew him to fale. mother sed that 10 days wood give her time to get ready. we have all got to wirk. then mother sed she wood have to warn father not to say ennything tuf and warn the children not to speak when the minister was saying grace and not to notice the new napkins and thing like that and that she had got to sweep evry room and wash all the winders and rub up the silver and the caster and the caik baskit.

when father come hom tonite mother she told him about having the minister to supper and father sed gosh what for. and mother she sed George that is a nice way to speak about a minister and father he sed why can't you let me take him down to old Eph Cuttlers and get him a stake and sum fride potatoes and about 4 fingers of fusil oil whiskey and it wood do him a pile of good. mother she sed i am ashaimed of you George for talking so. why cant you take it serius and father he sed it is serius ennuf and i am trying not to burst into teers over it. honest if you wood let me take him to Hirveys resterant it wood save you a lot of truble. but mother sed no we must do our part and father he sed gosh he suposed so but it was tuf. then father he sed i suppose you wont dast to bat out the flise if he comes. then Beany hollered for me and i dident hear eny more.

July 11, brite and fair. i have got an idea. me and Pewt and Beany are goin to talk it over tonite. we are going to have chicken and gelly and hot bisquit and custereds and cold ham and cookys and whips and lots of other things for supper friday nite. Keene and Cele are going to sing shall we gather at the river and theres a chirch in the valley by the wild wood. father wanted them to sing little brown gug how i love thee and we'll all drink stone blind when Johnny comes marching home and Sally come up Sally come down Sally come twist your heal around the old man has gone to town Sally come up in the middle but mother sed no they must sing good chirch songs.

July 12, Keene and Cele and i washed the winders upstairs today. i had to lug about 2 million pales of water. i asted mother what was the use of washing the upstairs winders for him as he wasent going to stay over nite. father he sed if we fed him two mutch he mite have the collick and have to be put to bed and perhaps stay 2 weaks. he sed we must be cairful and not feed him to hy.

July 13, brite and fair, we washed the downstairs winders today. darn the minister ennyway.

July 14, brite and fair of coarse. sunday went to chirch of coarse, also sunday school. more tuf luck. the minister cant come Friday but will come Thirsday so he will have a hoal evening with us. gosh.

July 15, had to raik up the yard. i aint been fishing hardly this summer. darn the minister.

July 16, or ennywhere else eether. today i had to cleen the barn and woodshed and pile the wood up neet. i wonder who they think is entertaneing the minister ennyway. darn him to darnation. i hoap nobody will ever see this diry.

July 17. we are all nerly ded. mother and aunt Sarah has been cooking all day. Keene and Cele have been practising hynm tunes and i of coarse have did most all the wirk. Pewt and Beany come over tonite and fixed up what we shall do to the minister. jest you wait and see old mister minister. i bet mother wil be glad and Aunt Sarah two. Tomorrow the minister comes. i bet he will wish he dident.

July 18, brite and fair. we have had a grate time. i never had sutch a time in my life. i gess nobody ever did befoar. everyone is in bed xausted but me. they think i am in bed but i am wrighting this. last nite me and Beany and Pewt talked over what we shood do to the minister. i told them what father done to old man Ellis and Pewt wanted to do that but i thot perhaps i mite not get the rite chair to put the bumblebeas in and if father set on them i mite as well run away to sea. then peeple has been knowed to tare off their britches when they are stang by the hornits and bumblebeas and if the minister done that it would be very mortifiing to my mother and my aunt Sarah and my sisters Keene and Cele.

so we desided that woodent be proper althoug we wanted to like time. then Beany wanted to put a live snaik in his hat, but we desided the snaik wood scare mother and my aunt Sarah and my two sisters to deth. then Pewt he sed less dig up some of those red stink wirms behine the barn and put a handfull in his hat. you know they smell so that you have to use soft soap and sand and scrub your hands 2 or 3 days before you can get it off. so neether of us wanted to tuch one.

then i sed mother is going to set the table and put on all the chicken and gelly and butter and cake and creem and everything and cover them with the fli screens and shet the doors and have nobody go in until super is ready. super is to be at six and she is going to have evrything ready at five and then they are all going upstairs and dress up in their best and curl Celes hair and ty up Keenes hair with a red ribon becaus her hair wont curl and dress Georgie and Annie and Frank and the baby and maik father put on a cleen coler and shert and black his boots and promise to be cairful not to say ennything that would shok the minister, so i sed less go in the kitchen and ketch about 2 million flise and put them under the fli screnes, and they sed i was a buster to think it up.

well at five oh clock the table was all set and it looked fine. i never see it look so good. so after the folks had went up stairs me and Pewt and Beany clim into the kitchen and cougt a bushel of flise and tiptode into the dining room and lifted up the screnes and put them under. after we had pretty near filled the screnes we tiptode out.

well father he came home and swoar when he had to put on a cleen shert and coler and i blacked his boots. i have to do evrything of coarse. that is what i am for so evryone thinks. mother had on her black silk dress with some lase round her neck and Aunt Sarah two and the girls was all dressed up and father two and they all looked fine. mother looked the best. she always does and Aunt Sarah the next. Keene sed i hadent blacked the back part of my shoes and that wasent enny of her business and so i told her to shet up and she made a face and run out her tung. then father he sed now if you two children begin enny of that you will go to bed lifely. so we both shet up. well we wated and wated and the minister dident come and we wated sum more and the minister dident come and i got scart, becaus if he dident come the folks woodent see the goke and i wood get time paisted out of me. well finally the bell rung and Cele went to the door. Keene was mad because she coodent and she started to run out her tung at Cele and then she remembered what father sed and she stoped just in time.

sure enuf it was the minister and he sed he was delade because he had to reprove thoughtless boys whitch were ketching small and innosent fish with sharp hooks. father whispered to me that is a hell of a reeson for keeping a man starving to deth and i laffed but nobody paid attension to me. well they all shook hands with the minister and Cele made a curtsy and sed tea is ready and we all marched out into the dining room mother and the minister first, then father and Aunt Sarah and then Keene and Cele and then the little ones and Georgie and i come last as i always do when there aint enny wirk to do.

well as soon as they got in i herd them all draw a long breth and then Aunt Sarah sed for mersey sakes and mother she sed for heavens sake and father he sed for goddlemity sakes and the minister he sed my greef what a disgusting site. well you cood hardly see the things to eat they was so covered with flise. then i winked at mother and sed

> god made the little fli
> and if you crush it it will die

and then i winked again but mother she dident laff back and father grabed me by the neck and sed did you do this devilish thing and he shook me till i cood hardly say yes, when mother made him put me down. then she sed what did you do sutch a dredful thing for and when i heard her voice i woodent have did it for a $1000, and i sed becaus the minister was all the time preeching not to kill flise and mother and all of us was all the time more you dident kill them the more you had to flap out and it got so that you dident dass to eat a piece of currant cake or blewbery bred for feer it wasent what you thought it was and mother she sed and then i stoped quick for i dident want to get mother in a scraip but she sed go on and tell it all.

so i sed she sed that if the minister had to fite with about leven milion flise evry day in summer for evrything he et or drank she bet he woodent preech god made the little fli and then the minister he sed but my dear boy god did make the little fli dont you reelise that and i sed and god made swallows and kingbirds and leest flicatchers and spiders, what have you got to say about that. i had him there but father sed no imperdence young man tell us all. so i went on and told all about it, what Pewt sed and what Beany sed and what i sed and what we done. 2 or 3 times father had to coff awful and wipe his eyes. he sed he got sum pepper up his nose some how he dident know how. when i finished father sed you go to your room and i will see you laiter. so i went up stairs and wated a auful long time afrade father wood come up and lam time out of me. well bimeby Cele come up and sed very solum father wants to see you down stairs in the dining room. so i went down and there they all set at the table with a new super ready and the flise all flaped out. all but the minister. father he sed sit down boy and have sum super and i sed aint you going to lick me and he sed not if i know myself and i sed where is the minister and father he sed he has went home mad. i tride to get him to stay and eat super with us and i tride to get him to go to Hirvey's resterant and he asted me if i was going to punish you and i sed that was a matter between the boys mother and father and i gessed they wood have to settle that themselfs and the minister was mad and woodent stay.

mother she sed i dont think he was mad George, i think he was hert. father he laffed and sed well if i had acted so i wood have been mad but a minister was hurt. ennyway he will lern something some day i hoap. then he filled up our plates and we et and et and et and father told the funiest stories i ever heard. we laffed so we cood scarcely eet. that nite after i had went to my room father he come up to my room and opened the door and sed Harry are you awaik. i had heard him coming and put out the lite and gumped into bed. i sed yes sir and he sed

    god made the little fli
    and if you crush it it will die

and then he shet the door and went to bed.

July 18, 186—-i bet that old minister wont come to our house again verry soon. we are going back to the unitarial chirch. they have got a new quire there and Keene and Cele are going to sing in the unitarial quire. it will seem kind of good to be there again, and there aint enny meeting in the afternoon only sunday school. i dont cair mutch about sunday school becaus they dont lern us mutch there.

today i rode horseback with Ed Tole. he has got a little red pony not as big as Nellie. it can go like time. Ed rides it without a sadle. when i ride without a sadle and sturups it nearly splits me in too, and hirts my backboan. today we raced. Nellie can trot faster than Eds but Eds can run faster. i woodent swap ennyway.

July 19, 186—-hot as time. today i met my uncle Robert. he aint my uncle Robert but is my fathers uncle. he is my great uncle so mother says. he aint half so big as my father. he is my grandfathers brother. my grandfather is dead. my uncle Robert aint quite. father says he is dead but dont know it.

well ennyway i met him and said how do you do uncle Robert and he sed whose boy are you and i sed i am George Shutes boy and he sed huh i hoap you will maik a better man than your father. i wanted to say sumthing sassy to him but if i had sed what i thought father wood have lammed time out of me. father always licks me for mispoliteness and imbehavior, so i jest looked at him scornful and tirned my back on him. he had went along so peraps he dident see me. i hoap he did. i bet my father is 5 times as good as uncle Robert. i asted mother and she sed i supose sum peeple wood say uncle Robert is best but i dont quite like his kind. i told father what uncle Robert sed and father laffed and sed i must not blame uncle Robert becaus after he was born they dident find it out for several weeks and so he got a bad start and hadent never cougt up. i wonder if that is true or one of fathers gokes i can always tell.

then father sed that Isac was a grate trile to uncle Robert he was so tuf, and Aunt Sarah she sed why George Shute you know that Isac never did a rong thing in his life and father sed no i gess he dident but if he had been aloud to go with me and Gim Melcher and Charles Talor and the rest of the boys we wood have made a man of Ike.

July 20, 186—-father has bougt 2 sheep. mother sed what in the wirld do you want 2 sheep for and father he sed he got them cheep becaus they dident have enny lamns in March. father says they may have sum enny time now and i must keep my eye pealed.

I have wrote a poim about our sheep.

> my father he has got 2 sheep
> he got them most almity cheep
> but if them sheep dont have no lamns
> he'll fill the air with feerful damns.

ain't that a pretty good poim. i bet Pewt coodent wright that or Beany eether.

July 21, brite and fair. i dont cair this time for it seems good to go to the Unitarial once more. i bet Beany is glad. i bet Pewt is two. i staid in the barn until chirch time feeding my sheep. Keene was mad and sed i smelt awful barny. Keene feels pretty big becaus she aint got to set in the same phew with me. Beany got stang by a hornet in the organ lof and one side of his face was all swole up. evry time he wood look out everybody laffed. so after chirch old chipper Burly told him he coodent blow the organ ennymore becaus he made faces and made the peeple laff. so Beany has lost his gob again. it was two bad becaus Beany coodent help it. we are going to get up a partition to get Beany back.

July 22, 186—-brite and fair. it is feerful dusty now and when we go across the street we stamp our feet and the dust comes up all over evrything. it is lots of fun when peeple are near you. went in swimming 4 times.

July 23. brite and fair. i had tuf luck today. first i got kept in the yard becaus i stamped some dust on 2 girls whitch was going down town in white dresses. mother heard them jawing me and come out and made me beg there pardon and she give them a brush and dusted them off and told me to stay in the yard all day. then this afternoon i dident have mutch to do xcept ho the garden. all the fellers was away fishing or swimming or buterfliing, so i dident have much to do and when old John Quincy Adams Polard went by all humped up over his cain i was picking buggs off the tomatoe plants and i jest coodent help it and let ding 2 joosy red tomatoes at him, the ferst whized by his head and he looked around jest in time to get 2th rite in the eye. well it squashed all over his face and he began to sware and to lam round with his cane and claw the tomatoe out of his eyes. then he come rite back to our house and i squat down behine the tomatoe plants. i was in a corner and coodent get out and he made for me with his old cain. i hollered for mother and she come out and stoped him after he had given me 2 bats and nocked down 3 tomatoe plants. well mother took him into the house and got sum water and towels and washed his face and promised to have his shert washed. then i had to beg his pardon. that made twice in one day. that is two mutch i think. then mother sent me to my room for the rest of the day. so i staid there reading for a awful long time and then i was trying to spit in the rane baril and mother caugt me and sent me to bed. a feller cant do nothing without being snached baldheaded.

July 23, 186—-today we wrote a partition to get Beany back his gob. it read like this,

mister Chipper Burley. Beany wasent making up faces last sunday when the peeple laffed. he was bit by 2 yeller jacket hornits behine the organ and he done pretty well not to holler rite out loud. most fellers wood have done it but not Beany. his face was all onesided and looked so funny that peeple coodent help laffin. his face is funy ennyway but peeple have got used to it when it aint swole up. Beany woodent have stuck his head out if he had gnew how he looked. he was not to blaim. so he wants his gob back and we hoap you wil let him come back.

Yours very respectively.

well we got a lot of people to sine. Earl and Cutts and father and Mr. Healy and Pewts father and old man Dow and evrybody that read the partition sined it and slaped their leg and laffed. sum of them roared and sed i gess old Chipper will take notise of that.

well then we drawed lots to se whitch wood read the partition to Chipper and i drawed the shortest one. i always do so i am not sirprized. i am going up to Chips tomorrow.

July 24. brite and fair. i went up to Chips today. he was in Boston.

July 25. if we dont have rane before long father says there wont be ennything to eat nex year. went up to Chips again today. he hadent got home from Boston.

July 26, i will never speek to Chipper Burley again. he has got the wirst temper i ever see. he gets mad for nothing. i never see such a man, i went up today. i met 2 or 3 men whitch sined the partition and they asted me if i had seen Chip and i sed no and they sed wel go up as soon as you can so i went up. a servant girl came to the door and told me Chip, only she sed mister Burley was in the greenhouse. so i went to the greenhouse and he was there with mister Busell and mister Alfrid Coner and old Charles Coner and Joe Hiliard. he asted me what i wanted and i told him and he winked at the other men and sed read it and i started to read it and i had jest got as far as mister Chipper Burley when he got mad and grabed it and toar it up and chased me almost down to front streete. i wish i gnew what he was mad about. i dident do a thing but jest start to read it. i bet i wont go there again.

July 27, 186—-rany and thunderry. i always thougt a girl with red hair and frekles wood taist jest loke dandylions when you bite them. i meen of course bite the dandylions. i meen when you kiss the girl. i dont know. some day i am going to find out.

July 28, 186—-i wunder why i wrote what i wrote yesterday. if i thougt ennybody wood ever read this diry i wood have toar that out. ennyway that is what i always thougt. i bet sum of the fellers know. but i dont. Beany has got his gob back. they coodent get ennyone else to taik it. his face has all gone down so it is not funny enny moar. at least it is not enny funnier than usual and we are used to that.

July 29, 186—-it was hot as time today. this afternoon me and Cawcaw Harding went up to the gravil to go in swiming and jest as we was jest ready to dive in a cold mist came up and we nearly froze befoar we cood find our close. i tell you we dresed pretty quick and hipered for home. father sed it was a sea tirn and sumtimes horses and catel has been lost and froze to deth by them and i had beter be cairful about going in swiming when it is too hot. i never know when father is goking. one day i asted him what the fellers witch lived in south America and Africa did for snow-baling and he sed that the snow was so hot sumtimes that they had to cool their snowballs befoar they pluged them at other felers or they wood scald them or burn them bad. i gnew that father was goking that time but the nex day in school i read in a school book that a man once froze water in a red hot cup. so peraps he wasent goking after all.

July 30 186—-i have to cut grass for them sheep evry day now and it taiks a lot of time when i cood be fishing. i never see such things to eat. always baaing for sumthing to eat. today they et a whole cabbije i hooked out of J. Albert Clarks garden, and a bushel of grass i cut over by the high school and sum carots and sum meal and hay and a lot of potatoe pealings and 2 peaces of lettis and drank haff a pale of water and tiped over 3 whole pales full. one is tame and follows me round. that is the old one. the young one is wild and if i dont look out wil butt me when i aint looking and where i aint xpecting it. once she nocked me over and i hit her with a stick hard. so now when i get in the pen she gets in the corner. she knows she cant fool with me. i guess not.

July 31, 186—-this morning we heard a awful baaing in the sheep pen and father called me erly and we went out. what do you think they was 3 lamns there. 2 was ded. the old sheep the one that i liked becaus she was tame was the one whitch lamns was ded. she was runing up and down and smelling of them and baaing. then she wood waulk away from them and look round and see if they was folowing her and when she see that they dident she wood come back and baa sum more.

father he sed thunder that is too bad we will have to berry them. i dont want your mother to see them. it wil maik her feel terrible. so i got a spaid and father took up the 2 little lamns and we went out behine the barn and father dug a hole and then we rapped them up in sum brown paper and berrid them. when we went back to the barn the old sheep was baaing terrible and runing from one end of the pen to the other end. her eyes stuck out of her haid and she looked at us as if she was asking us where her lamns was. father sed thunder this is tuf what in time can we do. i sed i dont know and he sed he dident supose i did he never gnew me to know ennything when it was asted. so he patted her head and called her a good old girl and i got sum grass for her but she woodent eat. the other lamm was all right but the first thing i gnew the mother sheep nocked her oan lamn over. jest butted it over. father sed hell and he was over the fence in jest 2 secunds. then he let her up and she backed into a corner shaiking her head.

then the lamn kind of teetered up to her wobbly as time and tried to suck and she butted him again and nocked him down and father grabed her by the back of the neck with one hand and by the end of her back with the other and sed now old lady you will do one of 2 things in about 2 minits. eether nurse this lamn or go down to butcher Haleys. so i poked the lamns nose under the sheep and in a minit it was sucking like a good one and wigling its tale like a snaik when you step on its head. the old sheep tried to butt and kick and get away but she mite jest as wel have tride to brake away from a steal trap. i bet my father cood hold a wild bull of bastem that the minister talked about if he had him by the neck with one hand and the tale with the other. i tel you that lamn had a good time. after he dident want enny more father put him in another pen and let the old sheep go. this noon he held her again. it took us so long that it was too lait to go to chirch. i bet i dident feel bad. after dinner father held her again. tonite he held her a few minits and then he let me hold her. she only yanked once but i held her as good as father.

August 1, 186—-this morning father dident have time to hold the sheep so he hollered up-stairs for me to get up and hold her. then i heard the door of the hack slam and i thought as long as father had went to the trane i woodent hurry and the nex i gnew mother was shaiking me and teling me that it was eigt oh clock and that my lamn was bleeting terrible. so i gumped up and dresed and run down and put the lamn in the pen and clim after it. the old sheep backed into a corner when i went towerds her and stamped her front foot and befoar i cood gump to one side she hit me with her head and nocked me flat. i gnew beter than to get up and so i roled over towerds her and got her by the legs and then i got a good grip in her wool. we had a regular rassel and she draged me all over the pen. i held on like a good feler and bimeby i got her in a corner head ferst. then the lamn woodent come to suck. i gess he was scart. i dident blame him for i was scart two. if i hadent been scart i would have let go so i hollered for Keene but nobody caim. i cood hear them ratling dishes and eating breckfast and i was most starved to death and i dident dass to let go of that old sheep. so i hung on and began to call the lamn. it wood baa and come prety nearly up and then run back. bimeby it come so near that i cood reech it but when i let go of the sheep with one hand she began to kick and strugle and i had another rassel with it. i was most tuckered out when she stoped to rest again. then i hollered for sumone to come but nobody caim. then i hapened to think that in the Swiss Family Robinson that the father was triing to ride a wild ass and it kicked and bit and rared and plungged and the only way to stop him was to bite his hear. so when he rared up strait he grabed his ear with his teeth and bit it throug and the ass got down on his feet once more and stoped kicking and biting and plungging and he never had enny moar truble with him.

so i made up my mind that when that sheep began to tare round again i wood try it. so bimeby the little lamn come up close and i let go one hand to stick the lamns head in place when the old sheep began to try to get away and i got both arms round its neck tite and grabed its ear with my teeth and bit as hard as i cood. well i wish you cood have saw what hapened. i never gnew wether she tirned a back summerset or i did. i gess we both did. she led out a baa and slamed me down on the floor and trod al over me and butted me over and tride to gump out of the pen. while i was on the ground and she was steping on me i caugt her by the legs and down she went and most squashed me flat and one of her feet trod on my head. you jest bet i hollered and then Keene and Cele and mother and Aunt Sarah come out and told me to get out of the pen befoar i was killed. i had been triing to get out ever since i bit her but she seamed to be evrywhere to onct. when they come she ran into a corner and i clim out. i was all covered with dirt and my nose was skined and my close toar. Keene asted me if i had ben playing ring round the rosy and mother told her that she must wash and mend my close for that before she went out of the yard. so i gess Keene wont be so smart another time. i went back to my room and changed my close and washed my face and hands and mother put some plaster on my face. then i had breckfast.

tonite i am so tired that i cant wright enny more. tomorrow i will tell how we fed the lamn. i have got so i can handle the sheep all right. Sam Dire done it.

August 2 186—-brite and fair. yesterday after i had my breckfast mother told me to ask Sam Dire what to do to fed the lamn. mother says Sam Dire is the lady from Philydelfia like the story of the Peterkin family in the young folks. when the Peterkin family in the magasine is stuck and dont know what to do they go to the lady from Philydelfia who tells them jest what to do. so mother sends for Sam Dire when she dont know what to do. so Sam he came over and clim into the pen and grabed the old sheep and held her until i got the lamn and it had enuf.

then Sam he went over to the blacksmith shop and he made 2 rings of iron. then he got a strap with a buckel and he put the strap with a ring on it round her neck. then he fassened a peace of closeline to the ring and run it throug the other ring whicht he had fassened to a beem in the corner and brougt the end of the roap out of the pen and tide it. so all i have to do now is to pull her up to the ring and ty the roap. then i get my gnee agenst her and she cant move. i done it at noon and at nite. she holds back when i pull but when i brace my feet agenst the side of the pen and pull you bet she has to come. that was prety good of Sam. tonite father nearly dide when i told him about biting her ear and mother told him how i looked. he went over and paid Sam 25 cents and told him he was a beter inventer than the man which invented hot water and i tell you Sam was pleased most to deth.

August 3, 186—-i think Lizzie Tole is the pretyest girl i ever see in my life. it looks as if Beany wood get her. still i am hoaping.

August 4, 186—-i woodent have ennybody read this diry for 2 million dollars. i am very cairful about it. Beany is a pretty good feller but there is sum things that no feller can stand. i gess Ed Tole likes me better than he does Beany but Lizzie dont. I wood ruther have it the other way. still i am hoaping. Beany may see sumbody he likes better. so may she. i hoap it will be me. i forgot to say that this was sunday. i tride to get father to let me stay at home to taik cair of the sheep but he woodent. he staid home himself to look after them. i dont think that is fair. they was a thunder shower this afternoon. it was after chirch of coarse. it was a ripper. it struck a tree up on Coart strete and split off a big lim. i have to wirk pretty hard cutting grass for them sheep.

August 5, 186—-i have to wirk harder than enny feller i know. all Beany has to do is to split kinlins and lug in wood and get water from the well with the old chane and windlas and that is always fun becaus a feller always splashed the water all over him and sumtimes the chane brakes and they have to fish for it with hooks and sumtimes things get in the well and you cant use the water for a long time and then Beany has to come over to my house. once a cat got drownded in Beanys well. Beany cood see it floating round but me and Beany was mad and he sed he never wood come over to my house again or speak to me as long as he lived. so Beany dident say nothing to his family but kep on luging in pales of water. bimbye the water began to smel bad and taist feerful and Beanys father xamined the well after about a week more and found the old ded cat and there was a dredful time and Beany got a licking and had to come over to our house for water until his well was clened out. ennyway we had made up. gues what we got mad about. i treted Lizzie to gibs and Beany got mad and woodent speak to me or to her. then he bought a prize packige of candy and got a ring that was wirth a grate deel of money and gave it to her and now she goes with Beany and dont speek to me. i am never going with girls again. ennyway me and Beany are all rite again.

August 6, 186—-brite and fair. Pewt is wirking for his father painting the Academy fence. he says he gets one dollar and a quarter a day. gosh i wunder if he does. Beany says Pewt dont get fifty cents a year. Pewt woodent wirk if he dident get paid. he always has got money too. so i gess he gets sum pay. i almost never have enny money xcept when i let my boat and bisness is poar this summer. i doant beleve i have ernt 2 dollars this summer. i think father had aught to pay me fer all the wirk i do. i am tired of that old sheep. i wish a dog wood come in some day and kill it. we all like the lamn. it is geting so it can eat grass a little. evry day i ty the old sheep out in the grass. i wish it was ded. evry time it baas i have to give it sumthing. i wood like to give it sum poizon.

August 7, 186—-hot and thundery. Cele is reading the bible throug. she reads a chapter evry morning. she is terible religius. she is a grate reader of dime novels. she reads all mine. father lets me read them. he says he likes to read them himself. it is all indian fiting. Cele has read Nat Todd the Traper and Billy Bolegs and Scalploc Sam and Mountain Mike and One Eyd Pete and lots of them. she says she likes the bible best. i dont beleve it. she has got as far as the 2th palsam. once father made me lern a palsam. he gave me 10 cents. i have tride to forget it and it is most forgot. it goes like this.

day unto day utterith speach and nite unto nite showeth gnowledge.

there is no speach nor gnowledge where thy voice is not heard. that is all i can remember now. once i cood say it all but i dident know what it ment. i gnew what the 10 cents was for.

mother dont believe it wil do Cele eny good to read dime novels but father says it will help her atain a hapy medium.

August 8, 186—-mother dont like to have Cele read dime novils. father dont cair. i dont cair much so long as father dont stop me. of course Cele cood read mine after i had got throug them, but Cele wont do that. she is two good for this wirld. it is funny. Cele is as stuffy as a bull dog but she has got a new England consciense, so father says, and if mother tells her not to read dime novils she woodent do it to saive her life. but if Cele thougt it was rong to read dime novils mother and father cood lam time out of her but they coodent maik her read them. she thinks it is rite to read dime novils but if mother tells her not to she wont read them if you cut her rite hand off. that is Cele.

August 9, 186—-me and Cele are reading Wild Mag the Trappers Bride. she has got to the nineth palsam now. she gets the novil when i am cutting grass for that old sheep and i get it when she is reading the palsams. i bet i can remember the novil beter than she can the palsam. i bet she can two. Keene dont read eether. she is reading Weded but no Wife in the New York Legger. i think mother dont like that eether. tonite mother and father had it out. father sed he thougt it wood be all rite for Cele to read novils but if mother sed no it was going to be no and that is all there was about it. Keene coodent keep still and sed it aint nice to read dime novils and mother sed it is wirse to read Weded but no Wife in the Legger and father sed that is jest dam rite Joey, he calls mother Joey, and so Keene has got to stop reading that story. Cele cried and Keene was mad. i dident yip and nothing was sed about me. i know when to keep quiet as well as the nex one. this is one of them times. after we had went out i told Cele i wood read it and tell her all about it but she sed no it woodent be rite and she went off balling and wiping her eyes. she red 2 palsams today to make up. i am glad i havent got a New England consciense. it is a awful thing to have when they is enny fun going. i hoap i shal never have one.

August 10, 186—-brite and fair. the ferst chirch is going to have a picknic a week from nex Tuesday. father says i cant go becaus i am a unitarial. i dont see why. i used to go to the ferst chirch.

August 11, 186—-sunday today. it raned hard all day. it is the ferst time i ever gnew it to rane on sunday, and i gess it is the ferst time it ever did in this wirld. I sed i wood like to go to the ferst chirch and sunday school but father he sed not mutch young man, but so long as you are so anchious to go to chirch you can go to the Unitarial with your sister Celia. i tride to get out of it but he made me go. so me and Cele went. this is one of the times when i dident know enuf to keep still. i am going to that picknic sumhow. unitarials dont never have picknics. that is the only thing i have got agenst them.

August 12, 186—-in 3 weks from today school begins again. i dont like to think of it. it is a shaim. i waulked down town with the ferst chirch minister Mister Borows today. he asted me why we dident go to his chirch enny more and sed that he missed my sisters singing in the quire. he dident say ennything about missing me. i told him we was all crasy to get back to his chirch and sunday school, only i called it sabath school becaus ministers always call it that and evrybody else doesnt. he asted me if we become crasy to get back about the time we heard of the picknic and i sed no not exackly then, for we had always felt like that way but we was more crasier when we heard of that. all he sed was hum. that can meen most ennything you know. i am going to that picknic sumhow. i wish that old sheep was ded. if i see a bear climing the fense to kill that sheep and take off her skin and rap it up in a neet roll the way bears do and then eat it, i mean the sheep and leeve the skin and i had a gun in my hand i woodent shoot that bear. that is the way i feel about her. evry time i want to go ennywhere i have to taik cair of that old sheep ferst.

August 13, 186—-i havent seen a show in Exeter for a long time. i wish i gnew how i was going to that picknic.

August 14, 186—-i was going fishing all day today and taik my dinner with me but of coarse i had to come back at one oh clock to feed that darned old sheep. i wish we lived in a bear country.

August 15, 186—-brite and fair. perhaps if i did i woodent dass to go fishing. ennyway i wish that old sheep was ded. i am still hoaping to go to that picknic.

August 16, 186—-we have had a terrible xciting time here today. if it hadent been for Cele we wood have lost our sheep. me and Keene fit hard with clubs and broomsticks and kicking in the ribs and pulling his tale but Cele done it. i shood never have thougt of it. but Cele did. father says Cele is a heroin. he says Cele has got some branes but that me and Keene has got moar curage than jugment. He says mother has got some branes two. i gess father was tickled to deth about it.

well this is the way it was. old Henry Dow has got a awful cros dog. when it aint tide he keeps it with him. today it got untide or knawed its roap and the ferst i gnew i heard Keene begin to screach and a growl and a kind of choking sort of baa. i was up in the barn lof, but when i herd that i come down pretty quick. when i got there old Dows dog had that sheep rite by the gozzle and had throwed it down. the lamn was trembling and baaing and Keene was lamming that dog with a broom jest as hard as she cood paist him and screaching as loud as she cood. he dident mind the broom stick enny more than a fether. i ran up and kicked him in the ribs but that dident maik him let go. i got hold of his tale and pulled and kicked but he hung on. they was maiking a awful choking growly noise. mother run out and then run back and i herd her pumping a pale of water and i run for the ax. jest as i got it and come out of the shed Cele come taring out of the house with sumthing shiny in her hand and throwed it rite in that dogs nose and eys, and he let go and began to howl and paw at his eys and nose and role over and tare round. people were running into the yard and mother come out with a pale of water jest as Sam Dire clim over the fence with a red hot iron in his pinchers and come taring up. the dog had scooted for hom howling bludy murder and when Sam got there he was so xcited he put the red hot iron on the sheep and set its wool afire. we wood have had roast lamn for dinner if it hadent been for mother who throwed her pale of water part of it on the sheep and part of it on Cele who got in the way. the funny part of it was that when we xamined the sheep we found she wasent hurt mutch. the bull dog had got his teeth partly in her thick wool and partly in her lether coller. she was scart about to deth and kep hudling up against us like a cat. Keene she sed she saw the whole of it. the old bull dog started for the lamn and that old sheep whitch had never liked the lamn gumped rite in front of it with her head down and the bull dog gumped and grabed her instead of the lamn. if he had grabed the lamn he wood have killed it to onct. tonite father asted more than 40 questions about it. he sed we al done splendid. that me and Keene showed grate curage but that Cele and mother showed grate jugment. he nearly dide laffing when he heard Sam Dire set fire to the sheep. he sed he gesed Sam dident want to lose his heat. father asted Cele how she hapened to think to do that and that is the funny part of it. sumtimes you have to laff at funerals. well Cele sed that in Scalploc Sam a bear had a deth grip on his dogs throte when Scalploc Sam he grabed his pepper pot and throwed a hanful of pepper in his eys and nose and while the bear was ritheing in agony and filling the welkin with horid roars and snarls and growls Scalploc Sam loded his thrusty riffle and slew him. slew means kill.

so that give Cele the idea and she done it. she sed she dident get enny help from the palsams. so mother is going to let Cele read dime novils if she dont read two many. then Keene up and sed that she had aught to be aloud to read Weded yet no wife but mother she sed no. so father give Keene 15 cents and gave me ten cents. i told him he had aught to let me go to that picknic but he sed he dident believe in eleven hours conversion i told him i had been thinking about that picknic for eleven days and he laffed and sed i would have to get along with that ten cents. i tell you we was all tired tonite. i think father had aught to let me go to that picknic. i am still hoaping.

August 17, 186—-today that sheep let the lamn suck and seamed to like it. she rubed agenst me and was as tame as the old one was. if she is going to ack that way i shall like her. Beanys father is going to let Beany go to that picknic. Mister Watson Beanys father rings the town bell and is the ganiter of the ferst chirch. Beany always has all the luck. i dont have enny. it is most time for that picknic but nobody aint sed nothing to me about it yet. i am still hoaping.

August 18, 186—-when i woke up this morning it was raining hard and it raned all day. this is the ferst time i ever gnew it to do that and the 2th time i ever gnew it to rane on sunday. today i split the wood and luged it in and fed the sheep and did all them things that i have to do and most felers dont have to do and then i read awhile and we talked about the bull dog and the sheep. then i rote a poim about it.

> one day in sumer in Au-gust.
> it was so hot we nearly bust
> my sheep was painting with the heat
> when a dog came taring down the street
> and then without delay or pause
> he gumped on them with teeth and claus

P. S. a dog aint got no claus to clau with, only nails and nails woodent rime with pause.

> he seezed that sheep by her white throte
> and shook her till she was all aflote
> he wood have killed her ded rite there
> when my sister Keene who you coodent scare
> let out a screech you cood heard a mile
> and laid on a broom in her very best style
> and while she was taning his mizable hide
> i give him sum feerful kicks in the side
> and squashed him almost perfictly flat
> but he wodent let go for all of that
> till my sister Cele came runing out
> with a scornful look on her hansom snout

(P. S. a second time. it is a kind of mean thing to say about my sister Cele but it is a good rime ennyway as long as i sed she was hansome i dont beleeve she wood cair.)

    and she throwed in that dogs face and eys
    peper enuf to make 40 Kyann pepper pyes
    and that dog let go and begam to yell
    and howl as if he was rite in hell

(P. S. 3th we unitarials say there aint no hell but i aint sure)

    and he made for home on the cleen gump
    jest as mother came out with a pale from the pump
    and old Sam Dire clim over the fench
    with a red hot iron and a munky rench

(P. S. again. fench is ment for fence. poits can do this whenever they have to)

    and he set on fire that poor sheeps fur
    and that was the best he cood do for her,
    but mother throwed that pale of water
    half on the sheep and 3 fourths on her daughter
    and Cele sed Sam you dam big lout
    just what in hell are you about?

(P. S. once more. my sister Cele never sed that really. she wood ruther cut her rite hand off than use such langage. but nobody but me will ever read this)

    and Sam sed looking verry wize
    i apoller-oler-ollergize.
    and then thinking he better not stop
    he clim the fence to his backsmith shop
    and oh how grateful that sheep must feel
    to me and mother and Keene and Cele.
    but old Sam Dire has went to his shop
    where we certingly hoap old Sam will stop.

(P. S. the last time. we really dont hoap so becaus we all like Sam very mutch. Sam is one of the best fellers we ever gnew. But i had to finnish the poim some way. ennyway Sam wont ever read it.)

There i think they aint many better poims than that. i bet the Exeter News leter wood put it in their paper if i dassed to let them. i bet Beany coodnt have wrote it. i bet Pewt coodent have either.

August 19, 186—-tomorrow is the last day before the picknic and i am still hoaping. it will be prety mean if i cant go to that picknic. i am stil hoaping.

August 20, 186—-hooray i am going to that picknic. i had almost given up hoap. mister minister Barrows come and asted me if i wood let my boat for the picknic. i sed i never let my boat to a picknic unless i rew it myself becaus i never gnew who wood row it and how they wood treet it and once they dident bring it back at all but after they had used it all day they left it up river and dident pay me and i had to go up after it and when i had waulked three miles up river i found it on the other bank and it was too cold to swim across and i had to waulk way back to the brige and then go up on the other side to get it and it took me most all day and the boat was all full of dried mud and ded hornpout and i had to spend the rest of the day in washing it out and dident get enny pay.

wel he sed they wood pay me well and wood treet the boat verry carifully but i sed i coodent trust enybody eether to pay for the boat or to take cair of it. so i sed i gess i dident want to let the boat unless i did the rowing and was there to look after it. i sed it was the only boat i had and that father was always telling me not to let evry Tom Dick and Harry have it jest becaus they wanted it.

he sed he wood assure me that everything wood be all rite if i wood tell him how mutch i wanted for it but i told him he coodent have the boat unless i went with it and he had beter get a boat of sumbody elce. he sed that my boat was large and safe and that nobody elce has so good a boat.

i told him that wasent my fault but that was the way i did business, so after awhile he sed well if i wood promise to do all the rowing that he wanted he wood ingage me and my boat and he is going to give me 50 cents. i only get 25 cents most of the time but i thougt i had augt to get 50 of him. so he sed all rite and i am going. when father come home i told him the minister had sed that if i wood come to the picknic and help row the boat he would give me 25 cents more than i usally got, and he sed i cood do it if he wanted me as bad as that. i dident tell father all i sed to the minister or all he sed to me. i dont think the minister wanted me very bad. i think he wanted the boat more. enny way he had to do it. tomorrow i am going to wash the boat out and i bet i will have a good time. Keene says she woodent want to go where she wasent wanted but i told her that when they paid me twice as mutch as i usally got it showed that they wanted me prety bad. so Kerry coodent say mutch to that.

August 28, 186—-it is almost time for school to begin and i have lost a hole week in bed and my life has been despared of. i dont beleeve enny feller ever was so sick as i have been and still lived to tell the tale. doctor Pery sed he never gnew a feller to go throug what i have went throug and live. it was that darn picknic that done it. doctor Perry says they aint a doctor in Exeter that dont lay in a lot of extry caster oil and rubarb and sody and a new popsquert and get a lot of sleep the nite befoar a chirch picknic. he sed that a collick from eating two mutch is bad enuf but when a feller is all swole up with poizen ivory leeves two it is wirse.

it is a very long story and i dont beleeve i can write it out all in one evining becaus sumtimes my head goes round like a button on a barn door so father sed.

wel the morning of the picnic i got up erly and washed out my boat and had it at the worf when the peeple come down. mother sed she dident want me to go unless i took sumthing for them to eat so she put me up a half dozen donuts and sum sanwiches and sum apple tirnovers and a little bottel of pickels. well i thougt they wood have enuf for all of the people without that and so i et it all while i was washing out the boat. i gnew i was a going to have a hard days wirk and i wanted to be ready and after i had hid the basket and had the boat reddy the peeple began to come down to the worf. they had baskets and pales and paper boxes and ice creem freesers and bottels and plaits and goblets and mugs and cups and brown paper packages of coffy that smeled awful good and made me hungry again althoug i had et a hole basket full.

well the minister was there with a long taled coat and a white neck ty and decon William Henry Johnson and decon Ambrose Peevy and Aunt Hannar Peevy and Widow Sally Mackintire and lots of them and evrybody was talking and laffing and stepping on things they hadent aught to step on and puting things in rong places and loosing things jest like old peeple always do.

the ferst thing they done was to pile on to the worf so many that the worf sunk down and the water come over it and wet most of there feet and they al screached and hipered up the bank and then begun

to blame me for it as if i had done it when i was in the boat and
dident tuch their old worf. and Mrs. Lydia Simpkins shorl went
floting down river and i had to row out and get it and she sed i had
augt to know better than to get too many peeple on a worf and wet
their feet and they thougt i done it a purpose. sum peple wood have
given me ten cents. she mite have thanked me. the minister was all
rite. he sed it wasent my falt. so they was more cairful nex time and
one at a time they tiptode acros the worf and got into the boats. i had
my boat full and al the women grabed at the sides of the boat and
hollered wen it rocked the teentyest bit.

but after they see i gnew what i was about they begun to have a
good time draging their hands in the water and setting one sided. it
made it awful hard to row but i dident say nothing but rew as hard
as i cood. i dident know until we got to the eddy woods why it was
so hard. it was becaus Thomas Edwin Folsoms coat tales were
draging in the water all the way. if i had gnew that i dont beleeve i
wood have sed nothing. they sung songs like lightly row, lightly row
ore the sparkling waives we go and rocked in the cradle of the deep
and come away come away theres moonlite on the lake and row
brother row the stream runs fast the rapids are near and the boat is—
-sumthing or other i have forgot. they always sing songs like them.

when we got up to the Eddy they got out and the decons coat tales
were driping over his hine legs so he took his coat off and hung it on
a lim of a tree to dry. then i had to lug all the baskets and pales up
the bank. befoar i went down for a second lode of peeple Mrs.
Dearborn give me 2 more sanwiches and 3 donuts and a drink of
lemonade for rowing them so good and when i had et them i started
down river again. it was bully to se how eesy that boat went after the
people was out. it was jest as eesy as nothing at all. i met all the boats
comeing up. they was rowing evry whitch way. the oars was
splashing and not keeping time. there was one man whitch thougt he
was a grate rower. he set in the back rowing seat and had 2 or 3 full
groan peeple in the front part of the boat and a little dride up woman
who dident weig more than a empty basket on the back seat and she
was triing to steer the boat. the bow of the boat was sunk down and
the stirn was up in the air so that the ruder dident tuch the water. the
boat would swing round and the man wood pull sideways till his
face was all one sided and jaw at his wife becaus she dident know
enuf to steer a boat, and she wood paw back that she gnew as mutch
about steering as he did about rowing. they were having a real good
time.

then i met Beany with 2 fat wimmen in the stirn seat and in the front seat Beany was up so high that his oars cood hardly reech the water and the boat was one sided becaus one woman was twice as fat as the other and the other peeple were leening over the side of the boat and Beany was sweting like a horse and mad enuf to bite a peace out of the bow of the boat and eat it and he was going about one mile an hour and his face was as red as Skiny Bruces hair. i set up and rew with long even stroaks and fethered my oars and dident splash a bit and the boat went on an even keel with little whirlpools when the oars came out and when i passed Beany the peeple in his boat sed dont that Shute boy row well, i wish he was rowing this boat. if he was we wood get there sum time today. and Beany was mad and i heard him say huh old Plupy is only showing off.

well when i got back to the worf there was sum more peeple wating with sum milk cans of lemonaid, and a freeser of ice creem and i was so hot from rowing so hard that i set down and brethed hard and wiped my face and held my head in my hands. they asted me if i was sick and i sed no only xasted becaus i am so thirsty my throat is dry. so they give me a glas of lemonaid and a saucer of ice cream and 2 peaces of cake and after i had et that i sed i felt better and was ready to row them up. they asted me how long it would taik and i sed if they wood set so the boat wood run even i wood do it pretty quick. so they done as i sed and i rew steddy by the gravil and the oak and the cove and the fishing bank to the willows whitch is haff way and they give me 2 glasses of lemonaid and when i had drank it i started again and rew stedy till i got to the last tirn when i passed Beany and the other boats that the old pods were rowing.

when i went by Beany he sed i bet you havent been way down to the worf old Plupe and the peeple in my boat sed he surely has and the fat wimmen in Beanys boat sed the nex time we come up we will get him to row us and not you Elbrige. i sed to myself low so they woodent hear me i bet you wont if i can help it.

well i landed my peeple at the bank and luged up their stuff befoar Beany got there. when he got there a awful funny thing hapened. Beany he give 2 or 3 long stroaks to land the boat and he done it pretty good for him. while the boat was running in Beany balanced in the bow ready to gump out and hold it. well when he done it and lifted the bow to pull up the boat the stirn went down so far that the water came over the side of the boat and the fat wimmen were setting in about six inches of water. well they screeched and tride to get up but they was weged in so tite that they coodent till 2 of the men gumped into the boat and yanked them up and you augt to hear them lay into Beany. the back of their dreses was sopping wet.

wel peeple had put up swings and fellers was pushing girls in swings and runing under them and sum were swinging in hammocks and sumone had bilt a fire and sum were setting the tables and sum were setting down on shorls and cushings and children were playing copenhagin and going to Gerusalem and it was a lively time.

i wanted to have sum fun but the minit i landed 2 wimmen that i had never saw befoar wanted me to go out with them to get sum flowers and leeves for their table and of coarse i had to go but as i was pretty well tuckered out i made them give me one more glas of lemonaid and 3 sandwiches. that was better than nothing and after i had drank it and et them i was reddy and we went off in the boat. i rew them across the river and we found sum vines with shiny leaves and a lot of yeller dazies and sum cardinel flowers and the wimmen made reaths of them one for eech plait on the table.

while we was doing this sum more people come and they began to make reaths and i helped them. bimeby we had enuf and we went back to the picknic with our arms full. when we got there they was a big crowd round sumthing on the ground and we run up and found that Beany had fell out of a swing and had hit on his head. he swang the higest of enyone when he fel out and if he hadent hit on his head it wood have killed him. it made him kind of squint eyd for a while and his head was on one side for 2 or 3 days but it dident hurt him.

miss Lewccretia Baley had spraned her anckle by steping in a hole and had to set with her anckle rapped up in a shorl. but i notised she et as mutch as ennyone, and Tommy Tomson had got a fishhook in his leg and had to have it cut out. evryone was having a good time and i cood smell the coffy.

after Beany was pernounced out of dainger and was able to crawl round and drink about 3 glases of lemonaid before dinner was ready, sum fellers is pigs ennyway, i had to row sum moar peeple up river for sum cardinel flowers. before i done this i got them to give me 2 creem cakes and a peace of blewberry pie. i aint like Beany always waiting to eat without wirking for it. a feller has to eat in order to wirk good.

well when i had et them i rew the people up river and when they wood see a cardinel flower they wood holler to me and i wood row the boat up to the place where the cardinel flower was and they wood pick it and holler over it and then we wood go on. the river was kind of low and the banks were steep and slipery where the cardinel flowers grew and Charlie Lane, the feller whitch was in the boat, had on sum white britches and we had got enuf and was going back when one of the wimmen sed oh see that splended one we must have that one. so i rew up and Charlie got out and clim up and got the flower whitch was a big one 2 or 3 feet above the water. when Charlie got it he turned round and sed

the rose is red the vilet blew
the pink is sweet and —-

and his hels flew up and he set down in the slipery mud and slid rite into the water, that is his hine legs went in to his gnees but he grabed the boat and that stoped him. his white britches were wet and covered with green slime to his gnees and the seat of his britches was black with mud. the wimmen nearly dide laffing and Charlie sed mersy sakes what a mess. most evry other feller wood have swore feerful but Charlie doesnt sware and is a good young man. that is why we call him Charlie.

well Charlie sed he gessed he wood woulk home and change his britches, he called them his pants, and so he got out of the boat and clim up the bank and started. i dident tell him he was on the rong side of the river becaus he dident ast me and i supose he gnew what he was about. the last i see of him he was going towerds Kensinton. while i was sick i sort of wurred about him but when i ast mother she sed he was in the store. he works for old Gid Lyford.

when we got back to the picknic old Mrs. Bolton had had a spell and the minister and Decon Sawyer was lifting her into Miss Susan Parkinsons caryall to drive her home. sum feller had throwed a teeny little bull toad in her lap. huh i shood think that was a prety thing to have a spell for. i never see ennyone have a spell. i wish i had got there in time to see it. Beany sed it was grate fun and elvrybody injoyed it.

Mr. E. O. Luvrin had been stang by a hornit on his underlip and evrybody had a good time looking at him. i don't beleeve there was ever a beter picknic.

42

the tables had been set and looked fine. our table with the reaths was the pretyest. well we all set down and evrybody sed hush, hush and the minister sed a long prair. peraps it seamed longer becaus i was most starved to deth. i had been wirking so hard and it was a long time since i had my breckfast.

well after the minister got through, we pitched in and et. i never had so good a dinner in my life. we had ham sanwiches and cornbeef sanwiches and tung sanwiches and pickles and milk and pickle limes and creem cakes and blewberry pie and chese and rasbery tirnovers and astrackan apples and balled egs and blackberrys and tee and coffy and sardeens on crackers and custerd pyes and squash pyes and apple pyes and gelly roles and tarts and coconut cakes and all the ice creem we cood eat, pink ice creem and white ice creem and yeller ice creem.

i et sum of everything they had. you see it was a long time since i had my breckfast and i had been wirking hard and mother had always told me to eat evrything in my plait and i wanted to ennyway. so i et until i coodent eat ennymore and most everybody done so two.

after dinner i helped clear away the things and then sum peeple went wauling in the wood sum slep in the hammucks and sum set down in cerkles and played gaims and told storys. they was one big cerkle whitch had the minister and most of the decons and their wifes and all the old wimmen and they was playing childrens gaims and hollering and laffing jest like children. old E. O. Luverin the feller whitch had been stang by a hornit on the underlip had told me to bate a hook and set my pole for a big hornpout or an eal. so i done that before dinner. i put a big steal hook on the line and bated it with the bigest grashoper i cood find, an old lunker, one of them kind that maiks a noise lika a nutmeg graiter and when it flise ratles its wings. then i unwound al my line and threw the bate out as fur as i cood and set the pole with a croched stick rite down in the sand by the boats. i was lissening to the peeple playing gaims when sum feller hollered Plupy you got a bite and i looked and saw that my line was tite and my pole bending. so i hipered down the bank and grabed the pole and pulled in. i had a big one on the hook and he pulled terrible, but i yanked him out and i pulled so hard that he went way over my head and rite in the middle of the cerkle of peeple.

43

it was an old lunker of an eal and when it lit on the ground it twisted and squirmed and thrashed round like a snaik and of al the screaching and tirning of back summersets by the wimmen whitch were fat and coodent get up quick, and of all the holding up of skerts and hipering for the woods by the thin wimmen you never saw in all your life.

and the men hollored and got out of the way of that eal as quick as the wimmen and one decon hollored what in hel and damnation are you trying to do you cussid fool, and sum of the others sed things i gess they wished they hadent. me and Beany was triing to get that eal of the hook. i got my foot on his neck and he squermed round my leg and got my britches leg all covered with slime. bimeby i got him off and into my boat, and when i went back old Mrs. Sofire Peezley was having a spell. i never seen ennyone have a spell before and it was very interesting. she screached and cried and then threw her head back and laffed and claped her hands together and roled her eys and gulped and swallered, and the wimmen were patting her on the back and making her smell of amonia botles and calling her dear and blesid lamn, and poar darling and talking to her as if she was a baby, and wimmen were coming back from the woods and saying it was a burning shaim and looking at me mad and saying i had aught to be in jale. and old E. O. Luvrin jawed me but it dident do no good becaus his lip was so swole that nobody cood understand what he sed. but i sed i aint done nothing what are you pichin into me for?

Then a woman sed you are the wirst boy in town and you are jest like your father was, and i sed i gess if you gnew what my father sed about you you woodent say much more and she tirned red and sed if that boy stays here i wont. it is a shaim to have sutch a boy at a desent picnic or with desent peeple.

then they all got round me and jawed me and the minister sed i must go home and i sed all rite if i have got to go i wil taik my boat, and he sed verry well take your boat and go. i am verry mutch disapointed in you. then i sed ennyway i want my fifty cents and they all sed dont you give him a cent he has been a newsense. then i sed it may be all rite to call a feller a newsence after he has rew about a hundred peeple more than fifty miles and luged barils stuff up the bank and made reaths and picked flowers and rescued peeple from drownding whitch dident know enuf to sit in a boat, but i aint going till i get my fifty cents then they sed if i dident go rite off they wood lick me and i woodent get my fifty cents.

so i got into my boat and rew up river. then i rew back and kept in the middle of the river and began to holer things to Beany. i gnew they coodent drive me off the river so i hollered to Beany did you see old Misses Peezley have that fit? gosh i bet she maiks old man Peezley stand round. peraps that is why he is baldheaded. Beany dident dass to say nothing.

then i hollered Beany did you hear old decon Aspinwall sware at me? he wanted to know what in hel and damation i was triing to do. that is prety talk for a decon aint it?

i shood think he wood feel ashaimed the nex time he speeks in prair meeting.

i cood see the decon talking to the minister xcited, and Misses Peezley was talking xcited two. but Beany dident dass to say nothing. so i hollered again to Beany did you see old Rhody Shatuck hold up her skirts and hiper for the woods? did you ever see sutch skinny legs? then old man Shatuck run down the bank and hunted round for a rock but i gnew he coodent find one becaus there aint enny rocks there and he tride to break a lim off a tree to plug at me and he hollered and sed he would brake my back, but i gnew he coodent get me and i hollered again to Beany o Beany aint it lucky the minister is married becaus all the wimmen is hanging round him and Beany dident dass to say nothing, but they all got together and talked and then the minister come down the bank and called me to come in and he wood give me my fifty cents if i wood go strait home but i sed not mutch i dont come where you can get a holt on me and lam time out of me.

well he sed i will not hurt you but i sed you sed you wood pay me and you dident and i cant trust you. he turned red as a beat and sed i am verry sorry that you acuse me of being untroothful but here is your money if you will come near enuf so i can toss it into the boat. so i backed the boat in holding my oars ready to row out if he tride to grab the boat or to gump in but he dident do eether but throwed the fifty cent peace into the boat and i started for home.

i gess it was about time for i began to feel pretty quear. my head aked and there was black specks before my eys and my face and hands burned like fire and smarted and my boans aked.

i gess i shall have to stop here for i hear mother coming up with my chicken broth and tost and am most starved to deth. father says i weig 2 pounds less than nothing and my arms and legs is jest like pipe stems or spider legs.

Continnude from the last.

August 29 186—-when i got home i hiched the boat and my head went round so i had to set down. then i got up and went home. mother saw me and sed what is the matter with your face it is as red as fire. i sed i gess the muskeeters done it. she asted me if i wanted enny supper but i sed i dident ever want to eat again but i wanted a drink of water. so i drunk sum water and went up stairs. then i begun to feel bad and caled mother and she come up jest in time. i was awful sick. father come up and Aunt Sarah and they held my head and run in and out of the room with wash boles and towels. o i was awful sick and mother sed for mersy sakes what have you been eating and father sed for goddlemity sake what haven't you been eating?

bimeby i felt a little better only my face and hands burned and itched. mother sed she dident like the looks of it and she never gnew a feller to be sick at his stomack with a red face and hands. so she wet a towel in cold water and put it on my face and hands and bimeby i gess i went to sleep.

sumtime in the nite i began to feel sick again and had awful panes in my stomack and i called mother again. this time i was awful sick again and father and mother and Aunt Sarah were verry busy for a long time. bimeby i wasent so sick to my stomack but my panes were wirse and father went for docter Perry. he was gone a long time before he come back with him. doctor Perry he took a look at me and sed poison ivory, so he got it did he. then he felt of my stomack and looked at by tung and felt my pulce and heard me grone and gave me a dose of castor oil and then he took out a little popsquirt the litlest i ever see and he sed i gess i shall have to give you a subteranian interjection. i thougt a interjection was a part of speach like alas and o and ah. ennyway that is what the grammar says.

but this wasent that kind for the docter run the sharp point of that little popsquert whitch was jest as sharp as a needle rite into my arm. it hurt like time and i hollered but after he had pulled it out i began to feel kind of lite and floty and the ferst i gnew the pane was gone and i dident know nothing more.

well the next morning i felt a little beter but not enuf to get up and not enuf to eat but after a while i felt wirse again and mother sent for doctor Perry again and he come and give me some more medecine and another subteranian interjection whitch put me to sleep again. the next time i woke up again i coodent open one ey and only see a teeny bit out of the other, but i felt better, only i iched feerful and smarted. doctor Perry laffed when he come in and sed i looked funny but not so funny as old E. O. Luvrin. he sed all the peeple whitch set at one table had it and had it wirse than i did, but i was sicker the other way.

he sed that all the docters had been up day and nite and always were buzy when there was a chirch picknic. he sed that if he had his way chirch picknics wood not be aloud enny more than prize fites and cock fites. he sed that the peple were pretty mad with me and thougt i done it purpose, but he told them if i had done it a perpose i woodent have been fool enuf to tuch the ivory myself, whitch was pretty good for the docter. ennyway i give him plenty of biziness. i suppose i hadent augt to have sed what i did about Missis Shatucks legs and old Misses Peezleys fit, but i aint sorry for what i sed about the old decon swaring. i hadent done nothing. jest cougt a eal. i must have left him in the boat. gosh when i get well enuf to go down to the boat he will be in auful smelly condition. i am sory i forgot him.

Well i had to stay in bed 4 days. most of the time i had web cloths on my head and coodent see nothing. Cele come up and read Wild Mag the Trapers Bride and a new novil Dair Devvil Dave the Dead Shot. she oferred to read the 92th palsam to me but i told her i dident feal strong enuf yet so she read 2 more chapters of Dair Devvil Dave instead.

Beany come over with a tame rat tide with a string. he wasent very tame and bit Beany 2 times. Potter Goram brogt his collexion of butterflise and a live green snaik. mother woodent come in until he put the snaik in his poket. the 2 Chadwicks Puz and Bug came in twise and fit for me, in the ferst fite Puzzy got a black ey and in the 2th fite Bug got a bludy nose. they was good fites and jest about even. i tell you they is always redy to help a frend.

Ed Tole brougt up his rooster and had arainged a fite with Gimmy Fitzgeralds rooster but jest as they was going to set them a going the old minister called to see if i was ded and when he found i wasent he made a long call and praid fer me and told me i had sinned deaply but wood be forgiven if i had faith. all the time i cood see Ed and Gimmy peeking round the corner of the barn and wateing till the old minister had went so they cood have their rooster fite. i was afrade they wood have it behine the barn where i coodent see it and i thout that old minister never wood go. while he was there he saw the bible open to the 92th palsam and he sed it is very grattifiing to me to see that you are reading the bible and i sed i wasent reading it becaus i coodent read ennything yet, but my sister Cele comes up and reads to me and he sed she is a very good girl indeed and i have heard she is very diffeernt from the rest of the Shute family. i sed yes sir. then he looked round some moar and found Wild Mag the Trapers Bride whitch was rite on the table. i wood have hid it only i coodent get it unless i piled out of bed and i dident think it was proper to get up in my shert tale befoar the minister. so i hoaped he woodent see the novil but he did and he picked it up and looked at it and read the naim and held it jest as if it was a bull toad or a snaik and then he sed are you reading this vile trash and i sed yes sir, and he sed how cood you read it with your eyes swole up, and i sed i cood see sum. he sed you jest told me you coodent see to read. i dident know what to say so i sed yes sir. then he sed awful stern do you meen to tel me that your sister Celia——and jest then mother she come in and sed i am afrade mister Barrows that we hadent aught to disturb our pashent too long. he isent verry strong yet.

and he said that is true Misess Shute but he has made some staitments about this improper book that i think it is my duty to look into and he held up Wild Mag the Trapers Bride and mother she sed it seems as if Mr. Shute and i are compitent to deside what our children are to read.

and he sed but my dear Misses Shute this is a verry improper book indeed and mother she sed have you read it and he sed god forbid i wood not disgraice my inteligents by reading sutch a book, and my mother she sed how do you know then it is a impropper book without reading it? and he sed how can a bok of the naim of Wild Mag the Trapers Bride be a good book and mother she sed she had read it and there was nothing impropper at all in it.

i dident know she had read it so when the minister had went off kind of stiflegged i asted her if she dident thing it was a riping story and she sed no she dident see how i cood read it but she had read it to see if there was ennything impropper in it and they wasent. she sed she only read it to see if there was ennything really rong in it. she dont care for sutch stories i am afrade. then she asted if i wanted ennything and i sed no and she went down stairs. then when she had went i clim out of bed and waived my hand to Ed and Gimmy and they come out with their rosters under their arms and set them a going and they hadent made more than a dozen gumps at eech other when in come old mother Moulton with sum gelly and custerd for me and she stoped the fite and jawed the boys and asted them if they dident know enny beter than to have a rooster fite in the yard of a poar boy whitch had nearly dide only a few days ago and Ed and Gimmy sed no mam we dident know he had been so sick and we woodent have did it and they picked up their roosters and went home and i skiped into bed prety lively for a boy whitch had nearly dide a few days ago. so when she come up i was in bed and i et the custerd and part of the gelly and it was bully. i wish she hadent come so soon. that wood have been a good rooster fite.

i set up most haff of the time today. tomorrow i am going downstairs. Fatty Gilman come down today and brought me 2 oranges and a red bananner. mother let me eat the oranges but woodent let me eat the bananner. i dont know what she done with it. i supose sumone et it. enyway i dident.

Aug. 30 186—-today i went out in the yard. it was brite and fair all day. lots of the felers come up and had a tirnament. first they had a match throwing green apples on a stick. Puzzy Chadwick throwed the furtherest. he threw one from my yard across the high school yard and it went throug a window in old Heads cariage shop. it was so far that when the men in that room piled out swaring they dident supose it was one of us and thy swore at John Toomy and 2 other fellers in the school yard.

Pewt was the next best. perhaps it wood have went as far as Puzzys but sumthing stoped it. what stoped it was a mans head. i dont know who the man was but when that apple hit him rite on the back of his head he throwed down sum boards he was luging into the shop and clim the fense and chased John Toomey and the 2 other felers way down south street. i gess he dident catch them becaus he swore so when he come back and if he had cougt them and licked them he wood have felt better. men always do.

so we dident throw enny more apples. so then we had sum rassels and the twin Browns and Potter Goram had a mach wigling their scalps and ears. Harry Brown beat on a scalp wigling and Potter on ear wigling. the 2 Chadwicks Puzzy and Bug fit again and neether licked.

then we had a spitting match. Ed Tole beat. he always does. then mother come out and sed i had been out long enuf. so i went in. i had a pretty good day.

September 1. brite and fair. it seams bully to be well again and to see the fellers and to go in swimming and fishing. i havent went in swimming or fishing since i have ben sick but i am going in in a day or too. i can eat things now whitch is better than enything. a feller cant do mutch unless he has a good apetite. father says there is one thing whitch has kept me back all these years. he sed that if i had had a beter apetite when i went to that picknic i cood have et nine pecks of stuff insted of only five. he sed he wood have to get the doctor to give me a tonick the nex picknic time so that i can do a gob that will be a credit to the family. he sed enny healthy boy witch can go to a chirch picknic and only eat 5 meesly pecks of food aint doing jestice to himself or his frends and he hoaps i will do beter nex time. he says he dont want me to make a hog of myself but he does want me to make a record that he can be proud of. he says i can be champeen if i only try hard.

i never know whether father is goking or not, but i think this time he must be goking. ennyway it wasent becaus i et two mutch that made me sick, it was becaus i got poizoned by poizen ivory leeves and that stuffed up my stomack. if it hadent been for that i bet i woodent have been sick. then going so long without ennything to eat and wirking hard dident do me enny good. they are still mad with me. i am sorry now i sed what i did. when a feller has lade between life and deth for 3 days he looks at things diferent from what they wood if he was well and was going round with fellers like Pewt and Beany and Whach and Fatty and Pop and Medo and Tady and Skinny and fellers like them.

So i have been thinking over what i have did and sed and i am very mutch ashaimed of myself. if enny other feller had went and sed things about my mother and sister or about aunt Sarah and my father that i sed about old Rody Shatuck and Misses Peezley and Decon Aspinwall i wood have felt like giving him a bang in the snoot. i wood have did it if he wasent two big, and if he was i wood have triped him up sum nite with a roap or plunged him with ripe tomatose or rotten egs when he had got on his best close.

but i needent be afraid that ennyone wood say ennything against my folks becaus they dont have fits and dont run round after ministers and dont hold up their skerts xcept when there is a mouse round and that is always at home where peeple cant see them. so i shant have to bat ennyone for that but that dont make enny difference becaus i have did rong.

so i have thougt it over and last nite when the band was playing departed days and the romance from Leclare in the band room i desided i wood wright a letter to all the peeple i had sassed and beg their pardon. it is pretty tuff to do it but it aint haff as tuff as being snaiked rite up befoar them by your father and made to beg their pardon. i have had to do this quite a number of times. so this morning when i woke up and had brekfast i remembered what i desided and i went up to my room and rote a lot of letters to peeple. i gess when father finds it out he will think i am pretty good feller after all.

it took me a long time to do it and i hated to waist the time becaus it is pretty near the last weak of vacation but i gnew i wood feel beter when i had done it and i done it. this is what i rote to decon Aspinwall.

decon Aspinwall
    Congregasional Chirch
        Exeter New Hampshire

dear sir i have been thinking over what i sed to you when i hollered to Beany about your swaring at me at the picknic last weak and i done verry rong and please to forgive me. of coarse it wasent so mutch becaus you swore so but becaus you are a decon of the chirch and speek in prair meating and so you hadent augt to have did it. but that is no xcuse for me to sass you. father sed i wasent verry mutch to blaim. he says he dont object to swaring but when a man tries to be a decon and plug ugly at the saim time it is the dam hippockrasy of it that maiks a man mad. i only tell you this to show you i was not verry mutch to blaim. but i am verry sorry i done it. you needent tell father what i sed, but i hoap you will try hard not to sware so another time when there is wimmen and girls and a minister present jest becaus a boy done what they told him to do and cougt a eal.

yours very respectively
    Harry Shute

i bet that decon will be glad when he gets that leter. i bet there aint many fellers whitch can write a better letter than that. i bet Beany coodent. i bet Pewt coodent eether. this is the letter i rote to old Misses Peezley.

Mrs. Sofire Peezly
  Exeter New Hampshire

dear Misses Peezly. i am verry sorry for hollering to Beany them things about you. when you had that fit i suposed it was becaus you was mad and i was kind of mad two becaus i had been cheeted out of my fifty cents by the minister, becaus i cougt a eal after they had told me to do it. then i remembered that my father had sed once that you had them fits when you wanted sumthing and kept having them until you got what you wanted and that he pitted mister Peezly. so i dident think when i hollered to Beany and i wish you wood pleese forgive me. it is a awful thing to have fits when you cant help it. mother says that peeple whitch have fits have to be verry careful not to get xcited. so when you go to a picknic again and enny feller throws a bull toad or a snaik into your lap you must reflek that a bull toad and a green snaik never bite or scrach and aint poizen. if you had gnew that at the picknic you wood not have had that fit. mother says that if peeple keep having fits they get wirse and sumtimes go crasy. so i hoap you will forgive me and will be very cairful not to get xctied. it is dredful to have fits and i am verry sorry for you.

yours verry respectively
  Harry Shute

there i think she will be verry mutch pleesed when she gets that leter. she wont think i am the wirst boy in town.

this is the letter i rote to Rhody Shatuck.

Missis Rody Shatuck
  Exeter New Hampshire

dear Missis Shatuck. I am verry sorry for hollering to Beany at the picknic last weak about your skinny legs. i woodent have did it if i had been well, but i had been poizened by poizen ivory leeves and the minister had cheeted me out of my fifty cents and everybody had jawed me becaus i cougt a eal and so i done it. if you had a hair lip or a squint ey or a wenn on your neck like old Nat Mason it woodent be so bad but it is a dredful thing to have such skinny legs as you have got and i am verry sorry for you becaus i have got skinny legs myself and the fellers have made fun of me ever since i can remember and it is awful to be made fun of all the time. if i was a girl i cood cover them up with my skert and nobody wood know they was skinny unless i fell down or the wind blew two hard or i pulled up my skert like you done at the picknic. so if i was you i wood be very cairful not to pick up your skert like you done at the picknic and nobody will know how skinny your legs is. sumtimes i wish fellers wore skerts but i gess i would ruther have skinny legs. so pleese to forgive me for what i done.

yours very respectively
    Harry Shute.

this is the leter i rote to the minister.

the referent minister of
    the ferst Congrigasionel Chirch

dear sir. i thougt i wood wright you and tell you how sorry i am that i sed the sassy things to you whitch i sed at the picknic last weak. i am also verry sorry indeed that i douted your word when you sed you wood give me the fifty cents. if you had been ennything but a minister i wood not have thougt you wood cheet me but i have heard my father say that ministers has so many things give to them and has so many old mades and fulish wimmen after them that they aint mutch to blaim if they forgets sumthings whitch they hadent augt to forget. you see i dident know you verry well and i thought you mite be one of them kind of ministers but i found out that you wasent when you paid me the fifty cents and done as you agreed when you promised not to grab me and lam time out of me. i was reddy for you and if you had grabed that boat i wood probly have rew so hard that you wood have been puled into the water all over. i am glad you done as you agreed and paid me. you were prety lait in doing it and i was not to blaim for thinking you wood not keep your agreement, espesially as the wimmen all told you not to pay me a cent. so i am verry sorry for what i sed and i think you done prety well for a congirigasional minister and i hoap you will forgive me even if i am a unitarial and done beleeve in hel as you do.

yours very respectively
    Harry Shute.

i bet when old mister minister gets that leter he will wish i had staid in his chirch. but it is two lait now. i bet they will all be sorry i left the chirch. it aint many fellers whitch are willing to oan up that they are rong as i have done in these leters. my granmother usted to say that a soft answer tirnith away rath. so i bet i have made sum frends by them leters.

when i got throug wrighting the leters it was almost time for dinner but i had a little moar time and i rote one mor to miss Tabithy Wilkins. she is a old made and she was xcited when i holered to Beany about the wimmen chasing after the minister and i dident mean her and so i thougt i had augt to tell her so she woodent wurry. so i rote her a leter two. this is what i rote her.

Miss Tabithy Wilkins
  Exeter New Hampshire

dear miss Wilkins. when i hollered to Beany at the picknic last weak about the wimmen running after the minister you thought i ment you and you got xcited. i thougt i wood wright and tell you who i ment. i dident meen you at all. i ment your 2 sisters Mary Ann and Unice and i ment missis Angilina Annis and Feeby Derborn and 2 or 3 others. i hoap you have not wurred about this. i rote jest as soon as i cood for i have been awful sick and lade between life and deth for a long time and coodent see ennything becaus my eys were all swole up by poizen ivory. i gnew you wood be glad to know i dident meen you, but i wood speek to your 2 sisters if i was you.

yours very respectively
  Harry Shute.

after i had rote that i got sum stampls of mother. she wanted to know what i wanted them for and when i told her what i had did she sed it was verry brave of me to admiit i was rong and i must feel verry happy over it and i sed i did and i et my dinner and put the leters in the post ofice and all i have got to do now is to have a good time for the nex 2 weaks.

September 3th, 186—-brite and fair and hot as time. i dident have enny chanse to wright ennything yesterday. i dident feel mutch like it neether. i dont believe enny feller had so mutch truble in 2 weaks as i had last nite. to hear father talk you wood think i was a bank burglar or a cannybile whitch kills and eats children. i have been jawed and licked and kep in my room and sent to bed without super, only Cele brougt it up after father had went down town, and had evry thing did to me jest becaus i rote them leters and i dont see what there was in them leters to make ennyone mad. i coodent wright enny beter leters than them if i tride a hole weak, and the peeple whitch got them is feerful mad with me and father says that posiably they may persecute me at law and i may have to go to jale for what i rote and father says i have got him into a feerful scraip becaus i told them peeple what he sed about them. but then he sed it so i dont see why he shood be mad, and what he sed is true and he says that evrybody knows it is true so i done see why he shood be mad.

the wirst of it is mother is mad with me two, that is to say mother aint mad xactly for she dont get mad but she is verry mutch displeesed with me and sed i done rong in wrighting to them as i did. i dont see why. ferst she says i done rong by hollering to Beany about them and she was glad i begged their pardon and now she says i done rong becaus i dident stop when i begged their pardon and not say enny more. of course i had to xplain things to them. ennyway i dont understand it now and i dont beleeve i shall if i have to go to jale for forty-five years. i wonder if peeple ever do stay in jale forty-five years. peraps i shall find out sum day. i dont care. ennything i sbetter than having evrybody mad with you. a feller mite as well be ded. i wish i was ded. if i was ded peraps sum of them wood be sorry.

well day before yesterday was a bully day. i went fishing in the morning with Pewt and Fatty Melcher and cougt 2 hogbaks, old lunkers and 3 pickeril and a big roach almost as big as the one i left in my jaket poket the time the folks thougt there was a ded rat in the wall of the house and got old man Staples to pull down the plastering.

then in the afternoon i went butterfling with Potter Goram and got sum splendid red and black ones on the nettle flowers by the side of the road. father he came home from Boston good-natured and was glad to see i was so mutch better and we had the roach and pickeril for supper and they was fine. after supper father went down town for sumthing and we was setting round the table. Cele had read the 95nd palsam and was reading Dare Devvil Dave the Ded Shot and i was wateing for father who sed he wood bring me a new novil from Fogg and Fellers store. Keene was reading the Fireside Companion, mother lets her read that insted of the New York Legger. Georgie was putting a picture puzel together and Annie and Franky and the baby had been put to bed when i heard father comin up the steps. as soon as he opened the door i sed have you got my novil and he sed the thing you will get is a thundering good licking insted of a novil and i see i a minit that he was mad. so i sed what have i done and he sed what in thunder did you wright that devilish leter to that infernal idiut Aspinwall for? and i sed i done it to beg his pardon and mother she sed i done rite. then father he sed that is a prety way to beg a mans pardon by telling him i sed he was a dam hippokrit. then i sed i dident say you sed he was a dam hippokrit i only sed you sed when a man tries to be a decon and a plug ugly one at the same time it was the dam hippockerasy of the thing that made you mad. i dident say you sed he was a dam hippokrit.

father he sed for goddlemitys sakes what is the difference? what rite had you to tell him that ennyway and i sed well you did say it dident you? and he sed of coarse i sed it and it is true but if you dont know enny more than to tattle evrything i say at home i will give you a good sound thrashing rite now and i thougt i was going to get it when mother sed wait George to father and then she sed to me what did you wright to decon Aspinwall and i cood remember all of it and i told her jest what i had rote and she leened back in her chair and begun to laff and laffed and laffed until i thought she wood fall out of her chair and Aunt Sarah she laffed almost as hard as mother and father he begun to laff and then we all laffed. i laffed becaus i see father laffin and i sed to my self it is all rite he wont lick me now. so i laffed. after we had stoped laffing mother sed how did you find out about the letter George and father he sed i went into Fogg and Fellers store to get your novil and while i was talking to Jack Fogg up come decon Aspinwall as red as a beat and sed what do you mean George Shute by calling me a dam hippokrit? and i sed i havent called you a dam hippokrit or enny sort of a hippokrit and he sed yes you have and i have it hear in black and white and he shook a leter rite in my face. so i sed i dont know what you meen. i havent rote any leter about you and he sed i know it but your misable son has ritten this atrosius epissle and you shall pay for it sir, you shall pay for it. well all the peeple in the store were lissening and i was a geting mad and so i sed well decon i know you aint drunk for you are to cussed meen to pay for a drink and so i gess you must be crasy but to keep you from going cleer out of your mind i will read the leter and i was sirprized. but i tried to smooth it over and sed now decon do you supose for one minit that i ever thougt that of you, mutch less sed it? and he sed yes sir that is jest what a man like you wood say and think two. well i kep my temper and tride to smooth him down but the more i tride the mader he got and finally he told me i was a defaimer of innosent persens and that he wood maik me proove it in coart. then i got mad and sed look hear you longnosed old vagrant, sue and be damned, but i have heard enuf of your chin musick and if you say 2 words moar i will smash that sankit monious old snout of yours so flat that they wont be able to see your ears. then i told him to go to hell and i come home. but it was the bigest fool performance to wright a leter like that i ever heard of and if you ever do ennything again like that i will tan the hide off of you.

i sed i woodent and i hoaped nobody wood say enny more but jest then mother sed i hoap you were moar cairful about the other leters and father he sed what have you sent enny others and i sed yes sir and he sed who elce did you wright to and i told him and he sed what did you wright to Missis Peezly and i sed i told her i was verry sorry for what i hollered to Beany and asted her to forgive me, and he sed are you sure and i sed yes sir hoap to die and cross my throte. and he sed what did you wright to Rody Shatuck and i sed i rote her jest about the saim as i had rote to Missis Peezly and he asted if i was sure and i sed hoap to die and cross my throte. and he asted me what i rote to the minister and i sed i asked him to forgive me becaus i douted his word and for sassing him and he sed are you sure and i sed hoap to die and cross my throte.

then he asted if i rote the same to the other peeple and i sed yes ser and he sed well thank the good lord you had more sence than you did when you rote the leter to old Aspinwall. and i sed yes sir I am glad i had so i thougt i was all rite when the door bell rang kind of mad. i can always tell how a person feals when he rings our doorbell and when he neerly pulls it out i know he is mad. i felt as if sumthing was going to hapen jest then.

well Cele went to the door and i heard a woman asing if father was in and i reconised Misses Peezlys voice and i gnew she was mad and i wondered what she was mad for. so father he went in and i cood her her yapping away at him and cood hear father talking but coodent hear what they was saying. mother sed i hope you told your father the truth and i sed yes mam. bimeby father come in and called mother and she went in and i cood hear her talking. jest then the door bell rang and Cele let in old Rody Shatuck and a minit afterwerds in come Angelina Annis and Unice and Mary Ann

Wilkins and Feeby Derborn all of them jest mad enuf to fite. i cood tell they was mad by the way they asted for father. i tell you i got fealing prety sick but i coodent see what they was mad about. when they went into the parlor you wood have thougt it was a chirch meating when they was voating for the carpet in the vestry. evry woman talked to onct jest as loud as they cood. i never head such a noise in my life before. bimeby father come in and told me to come in and told me not to say a word unless to answer questions that he asked. i hated awful to go in but i had to. when i got in they was all there with there faces as red as beats and mad enuf to bit spikes. Rody Shatuck called me a misable brat and old Missis Peezly called me a low minded retch and made a mosshun as if she was going to paist me one with her old umbrela, but father told me to set down in a chair by mother then Angelina sed to mother that she augt to be ashaimed of herself for incurageing me in my criminallity. that is what she sed but i dident know what she ment. but father who had not yipped a single yip sence i went in sed loud now look hear Misses Shatuck i want you to understand that you must keep Missis Shute out of this discussion. you can say what you like to me or about me and when you are all through i may have sumthing to say but if ennyone of you say a word disrespectful to her why then we will stop this thing to onct. Now if you understan that go ahead. well i gess they understood it for of all the talk you ever heard, you wood have thought to thousand hens was cakling. they jest give it to me and father. father looked stern and serius but i thougt i cood see sumthing in his eys that looked like he wanted to laff, but mother dident look a bit like laffing. bimeby when they had talked about a hour it seamed to me they stoped. then father sed now young ladies i am a grate deel older then you are and have tride to look at the matter on both sides. why father aint within a most a hundred years so old as eny of them but he gnew how to pleese them. mother looked mad but father went on. as for you Missis Peezly nobody here ever heard of you having fits or ennything else. i goke a good deel to home here and i never goke about peeple i dont like. it is always about peeple for which i have the greatest respec and liking. i may have sed sumthing like what he sed and if i did i hadent augt to have did it, and woodent have did it if i had suposed that this boy woodent have gnew better than to have took it serius. i beg your pardon verry sincerely and this boy must do it two. so father he done it and i had to do it a 2th time. well she told father she was sorry she lost her temper with him for evrybody sed he was a perfick gentleman, but she still thougt the boy had augt to be punished verry sevearly for mottifiing her so. father he sed she mite be very sure he wood attend to that and he glore at me when he sed it as if he wood cut me into 40 peaces and she sed good nite to father and good nite to mother and mother looked at her as if she wasent there and old Missis Peezly tirned red and snifed and went out stifleged.

then father he sed to Rody Shatuck now Missis Shatuck the last thing in the wirld that a yung lady shood be ashamed of is to be slite and graiceful. that is one of the menny things you had augt to be proud of. there isnt a fat woman in this town whitch dusent envy you for your graice and activity. of coarse the boy was very infortunate in his choice of words but i asure you that the only thing he did was to call two publick atension to your verry atractive figure. i am real sorry i was not there to taik advantage of a most unusual oportunity. and then old Rody gigled and sed she had been told she had a fine figure but she dident like to be told like i told it and father glore at me again and sed it woodent happen again and she sed goodnite to father and to mother and mother looked at her as if she wasent there at all and she tirned red and snifed and went off stifleged like old Missis Peezly.

then father sed to Mary Ann and Unice Wilkins and Feeby Derborn. young ladies there probly aint enny peeple that do as mutch for the moral uplif of the chirch as those devoted young wimmen whitch do so mutch to help the minister in his menny duties in the chirch and parrish and when the history of the chirch is rote you young ladies will occupy a very high place on the role of onner. they always is and always will be peeple whitch is consoomed with gelousy and probly sum one has sed things and my son has heard them. but i am sure young ladies whitch is so kind harted as you have shew yourselfs to be will not be two sevear on a boy whitch at the time was sufering from poizen ivory and over eating and as for his part he wood punish him sevearly for saying what he did.

so they sed if he wood do that it wood be all rite and they sed it was a pleasure to talk with a man who was so willing to do rite and to maik others do rite and father sed it was a pleasure to meat and talk to ladies of their standing in chirch and in society and he shook hands with them and they sed good nite to father and to mother and mother looked at them jest as if they wasent there, and they all tirned red and snifed and went off mad as time and jest as stifleged as the others.

well after they had went father looked at mother kind of funny and scrached his hed and sed well Joey, he calls mother Joey, you have got about as mutch tack as a fire alarm on resurexion day and mother sed George Shute do you realy mean to say that you are going to whip him for lying to you after what you have sed to them wimmen? and father laffed and sed he had to do sumthing to teech me a lesson and that one moar nite like this wood send him to a mad house. and mother told him he lide to them wimmen wirse than i had lide to him and he sed it wasent lies it was dipplomercy and if she had enny tack he wood have had them gnitting sox and mittens for him, and mother snifed two.

so then he took me up stairs and licked me. not verry hard but moar than i desirved. but the wirst was that i cant go out of the yard for 3 days and nex weak is the last weak of vacation. i think it is prety meen to treat a boy so whitch has lade between life and deth for 3 days. i always get the wirst of it when i try to be good.

i never will try to be good again if i live a million years.

September 4, 186- brite and fair. it mite jest as well rane as not. i cant go out of the yard today and none of the fellers have been up. i saw Beany ride by on Jo Palmers back. i hollered at him but he dident look. then Pewt went down throug the high school yard with 2 oars over his shoulder. me and Pewt aint so frendly now becaus old man Purinton has bougt 2 boats, new ones and is leting them to peeple for less than i get for mine. he has painted them all white with a red rim and a picture on the stirn and they dont enny peeple want my boat. i wasent mad with Pewt but he feals so big over his old boats that it maiks me sick.

ennyway he mite have come over to see me when i was sick and laid between life and deth 3 days. sum other peeple mite have come. Lizzie Tole was one of them. if it had been Beany she wood have went to see him.

i read in a book onct how a feller had a girl whitch took up with another feller whitch had a fine horse and buggy and a silver mounted harnis. so this feller told her he had lost all faith in wimmens consistency and had put them out of his life for ever. so the girl laffed and told him all rite she dident cair. so he went away with his hart curroded with bitterniss and went to wirk in a hotel. He wirked so hard that in 3 years he oaned the hotel and had money in the bank. then the girl rote him that she had always luved him and never had luved the other feller but he rote her that the dye was cast, he shood never marry. and he never did, so his children never gnew a mothers cair.

so i shall never marry like that feller who dident and all on account of Beany. sumhow i cant get mad with Beany. i had augt to menny times and keep mad two but i cant do it.

September 5, 186—-i got up erly this morning befoar father went to Boston and took cair of Nellie and swept out the stable and luged in the water and split a lot of wood and blacked fathers boots and set up and had breckfast with him. i was hoaping he wood let me go out of the yard. but he dident say nothing about that but did say i had got to get up evry morning befoar he goes away and do my chores i done them so well this morning. i thougt that was a prety mean thing for him to do. i wished i hadent got up. well tonite father he caime home mad and sed i was the bigest fool he ever see. he sed i had blacked his boots with stove polish and evrybody laffed at him.

so i wont have to get up. i had to black his boots over 2 times with Day and Martins blacking befoar i cood get them to shine. it was a awful long day in the yard. Beany brougt his black and tan terrier over and we got Frank Haines dog over and had a fite but jest as they were going good mother come out and poared a pale of water on them and they run off prety quuick. neether licked. that is always the way. sumbody always stops the good fites.

it was Saterday nite and after i had luged in about a milion pales of water and filled all the tubs for the folks to taik there baths in father he sed to mother, Joey, he calls her Joey, becaus her name is Joanna. sumtimes when father wants to plage her he calls her Johanna with a h and says she is irish. she dont like that becaus she is inglish. mother came to America when she was 3 years of aig and so she doesent remember verry much about ingland. father says mother dont understand gokes becaus she is inglish and mother says she is glad of it becaus a good menny of fathers gokes hadent augt to be understood by ennybody. when she says that father always laffs and says she is a goker herself sumtimes.

well i forgot what i was a going to say becaus when i wright about my father and mother i dont think about ennything else they are so bully. My father was the best fiter in Exeter or ennywhere elce. Ed Thursten told me that once he and father went down to newmarket and a feller in the hotel tride to lick father and father hit him a old he one in the snout and gnocked him up 2 flites of stairs and round 3 corners befoar he stoped. i bet they aint many fellers whitch cood do that. ennyway Ed was there and seen him do it and he says he can show me the hotel and the stairs and the corners he went round and the big dent in the wall where he stoped. so i gess it must be so. i bet Beanys father coodent do it. i bet Pewts coodent eether.

evrybody likes father and calls him George and he gokes with them and gets them to say funny things and then he laffs and evrybody laffs. so he dont never have to fite now. i am glad of it for i shoodent like to se father fite even if he can lick evrybody.
gosh it is funny i forgot what i was going to say. you see i think father and mother is about the best peeple in the wirld. i dont know whitch is best. father says mother is wirth 500 of him and he augt to know becaus he has gnew her longer than i have.

well father sed well Joey, he calls her Joey, how has the boy behaived himself today and mother sed he has done verry well indeed. so father he sed to me what do you say if we go in swimming at the gravil and i sed all rite i wood like to. so we went down to the boat and i rew him up to the gravil and we went in and had a grate swim. father dont like to have me swim under water. he says i stay under so long that he gets scart for fear that i wont never come up. after we got back home he let me go down town with him and after he had been to old Tom Conners store and old Nat Weeks and old Josh Getchels and Gid Lyfords we went into Fogg and Fellows store and father bougt a new novil for me. the naim of it is Grissly Ike the Scalp Lifter. i bet it is a riper. i havent read it yet becaus father sed as long as he let me go out befoar my tirm of imprisenment was over i had got to let Cele read it first. so she read it most all the evining. she only read one palsam tonite. she aint so religus as i thougt she was when they is a new novil round.

September 6, 186—-brite and fair to-day and cool. it feals like autum. i tell you i dont like to have the summer go. one weak from nex munday school begins. i hait to think of it. we will have to do the old xamples about A. and B. and how many squaire feet there is in 4 ackers 2 roods and 28 rods and New Hamshire is bounded on the north by Maine on the east by long ileand Sound on the south by Rode Iland and Conetticut and on the west by New York, and the capital of Tennysee is Tallyhassy and the capital of New York is Oswego and things we lerned last year. sumtimes i feal like saying to old Francis, who sed it aint, but i know if i did he wood lam time out of me. well i have got one moar weak. i hoap i wont be kep in enny more. i cant spair a single minit.

went to chirch today. the quire coodent sing becaus sumthing was rong with the organ. only the squeel keys wood go and they went as loud as a steam whistle. the base keys woodent maik a single yip. old Chipper Berley clim into the organ after chirch was over and found that sumbody had stufed a old pair of overhals and a old hat all spatered with paint into the big pipe. Chipper told Beany he done it and Beany he sed he dident hoap to die an cross his throte and then Chipper he held up the overhals and the hat and they both had I. M. Watson rote on them and so Beany has lost his gob this time forever so Chipper sed and he waulked Beany out by the ear. Beany told me honest he dident do it. he sed he pumped jest as hard as he cood becaus he dident want to let the wind go out. Chipper sed the reeson he pumped so hard was becaus he gnew that all the wind wood go into the squeel keys and sound awful. Beany feals prety bad over it becaus he needed the money. he has bougt sumthing at old Bill

Morrils gewelry store. I knew what it is two and who it is for but Beany dont know i know. Beany will feal prety cheap if he has to give it back to old Bill. praps she wont give it back to Beany. then Beany will be in a scraip. ennyway if she wont give it back Beany wont never forgive her. i hoap she wont. it will be tuf on Beany.

September 7, 186—-Beany is fealing prety bad. he asted me if i cood lend him a dollar. honest i coodent becaus i aint got it. he says he has got to get a dollar ennyway. i lent him 40 cents so he aint got to get but 60 cents moar. he tride to get a gob today poasting bills but Cris Staples got it. then Beany he went up to Chipper Berleys to get his pay and Chipper told him he was lucky not to get arested for distirbing a religus meating. so Beany dont know what to do. he aint got ennything to sell and i aint eether. he tride to borrow it of Pewt but Pewt sed he dident have it.

September 8, 186—-they is a circus coming to town next Friday. it was going to be in Portsmouth but there was another circus got the the circus grounds ferst and so they are coming to Exeter. me and Pewt and Beany are going to get a gob poasting bills. the bill poaster was in town today with a red and blue and gold cart with 2 calico horses and put up the big bills. he only had 2 big ones and dident have enny others and cant get them until Wensday nite and he wants me and Pewt and Beany to put them up in the nite so that when the peeple get up in the morning they can see them the ferst thing. the way he hapened to get us is becaus Beanys father and Pewts father is painters and paper hangers and so they went to them and they wodent stay up all nite to do it and then he asted if they was enny boys to do it for a dollar a peace and a ticket and so we got the gob. we cant tell ennyone jest what we have got to do but it is bully. he told us that we was to put the pictuers up in the rite places to make a show and atract the attension of the peeple. where they cood see them the best. so we are going to do it. he says the secrit of poasting bills is to get them in the rite places. he give us a list of the pictures. these are them. the hippotymus the behemuth of hoaly rit. the boar constricter whitch can crush and swalow a hole dear or oxx at one meal. the hieener that by stelth repairs to the graive yards at nite and digs up the bodys of the ded and devours them. Jo Jo the dog face man the ofspring of a babboon and a aborrygine, the most repullsive haff human being in the wirld. the stork which brings blessings to the householes in the shape of babies. the cheater or hunting lepard. the spider munkey, and the tapir and the geraft. Pewt has got the list so peraps i havent rote them all rite. we are going to meat and deside where to poast them up as soon as Pewt gets them. peraps tomorrow.

Sept. 9, 186—-rany today and cold as time. i tell you it ranes and blows. Aunt Sarah says may be it is the equinoxious storm. that usually comes on the 22th. i hoap it wont rane Wensday nite. we cant poast up bills in a rane storm and if we dont poast up them bills we dont get no dollar and no ticket and what will Beany do then? Beany is in a tite place. if he cant get that dollar he has got to get that present back from Lizzie Tole. if she wont give it back then Beany may have to go to jale and he wont never forgive her. if she has to give it back she will be mad with Beany forever and ever. i almost hoap it will rane. no i dont eether. it will be two tuf on Beany. what ever Beany has did to me i like him and i hoap it wont rane and that Beany will get his dollar. i cant be mutch fairer than that can i?

this afternoon we went up in the barn on the hay, me and Pewt and Beany and talked over where we are going to poat up the bills nex Wensday nite tomorrow. it raned so that Pewt dident dass to bring over the bills. they are in his shop all roled up in a role as big as my leg and tide tite. so we looked at our list and we are going to put the picture of the cheeter on decon Aspinwalls house. he is the bigest cheeter we know and everybody says so.

the stork we are going to put on Mrs. Clarisser Dorsons front door. Pewt says he heard his mother say that the dorsons xpect a baby pretty soon. so we all agreed that wood be the place to put it.

we all got jawing about where we shood put the picture of the elefant. Beany thougt it had augt to go on Horris Cobbs front door. Pewt thougt it had augt to go on old mister Gechels store and i thougt it had augt to go on Fatty Frogs house. Horris Cobb is the fattest man in town but he aint tall. odd mister Gechel is feerful tall, almost ten feet i gess but he aint verry big as Fatty Fogg is lots taller than Horris and 3 times as big round as old mister Gechel. so we decided to put the elefant on Fatty Foggs house and the Giraft on Gechels house.

the hieener we are going to put on the berrying ground gait rite under where it says we are all passing away. you know the hieener digs up people and devours them and Beany says that will go well with the sine. that was a good one for Beany. i bet that circus man will say we are prety smart felers.

the howling munkey we are going to put on the Methydist parsonage. the reverent Josiar Higgins has got white whiskers on his throte jest like the howling munkeys and i bet he can howl as loud sundays. so that is the rite place for that picture. i never gnew befoar how mutch beter it is to have things did rite.

we are going to put the picture of the tapir on my uncle Gilman's house. Pewt thougt it had augt to be put on Ikey Blums house only Ikey aint got any house and his shop is not on enny street. Ikey has a old plug horse and colects bones and rags and iron. he has the longest nose i ever see. it goes way down over his mouth. i dont see how he can eat. my uncle Gilman has got the next longest nose. his nose is a good deal biger than Ikeys but it aint so long. but uncle Gilman is lucky becaus he has got a house to put the picture on. he can blow his nose so it sounds jest like a cornet. not so good as Bruce Briggam can play the cornet but pretty good.

i bet he will be pleesed that he beat Ikey and Ikey will be mad, but nobody can have evrything in this wirld.

the picture of the boar constricter we are going to put on the front gait of old decon Eberneaser Petigrew. he goes to all the chirch supers and eats moar than enny man there. one time Charlie Folsom the resterant man whitch makes clam chowder wanted to see how mutch old Eben cood eat and he invited him in and made a hoal wash boiler full of chowder. Charlie sed he put in a peck of clams and 2 galons of milk and a lot of potatoes and onyiuns and he invited old decon Petigrew in and he et and et and et and et. Charlie begun to get scat for feer he wood bust. bimeby he stoped eating becaus he coodent hold enny moar. he had et all but about 4 quats. Charlie dident sleep enny that nite he wurrid so about decon. he thougt sure he wood die befoar morning. so he got up erly the nex morning and come down town. when he went by Ebens house he looked up to see if there was enny craip or a reath on the door. there wasent so he gnew he hadent dide but he gessed he was pretty sick. well what do you think when he got to his resterant there stood old Eben all rite wateing for him and he told Charlie that if he dident want the rest of that chowder he wood take it. so Charlie he give it to him and he says he must be jest like a boar constricter.

father has always told me to do evry thing rite that i attempt to do. he tells me that all the time. i gess he will find that i can do things rite as well as the nex one. tonite when we come out of the barn it had stoped raning and the sun come out i hoap it will be good wether tomorrow and nex day two. Pewt is going to make 2 buckets of paist. me and Beany are to get the flour for it and Pewt makes it. he knows how better than we do. he and Beany fernish the brushes to put on the paist. i fernish a lantirn if it is two dark.

September 10, 186—-brite and fair and jest bully wether. i got up late today and i am glad of it becaus i have a hard days wirk tonite, father told me this morning that i must distinkly understand that there aint going to be no fooling tonite but jest wirk. i prommised we woodent do nothing but wirk and put the bills in the best places so as to pleese evrybody. that is what the circus man told us not to do enny damige and not to get ennyone mad but to put the bills where they will attrack the most atension. and that is why he is to pay us so mutch money and give us a ticket apeace to the show.

after breckfast i split up enuf wood for today and luged in 2 pales of water and went over to Pewts. Beany was there and we opened the role of pictures and they were old lunkers. gosh the howling munkeys looked jest like the reverent Josier Higgins and the cheeter looked kind of slanty eyd and meen like Decon Aspinwall. the boar constricter was swalowing a live cow hoal. i bet peeple will laff. and the tapir honest he looked kind of like my uncle Gilman.

well we are going to go ferst over the river to uncle Gilmans and then to old mister Gechel and then to Pettigrews and then to Clarisser Dorsons and then to Decon Aspinwalls and then to the reverent Josier Higgins and so on. Pewt thinks it will taik 2 hours to do it good so they cant be toar down if we done it with tacs ennybody whitch dident like it cood yank it off eesy but if we paist it on with a little gum arab in it, it will have to be scrope off with a gnife. so Pewt says and i gess he knows, we carried up 2 paper bags of flour and Pewt made 2 buckits of paist. we paisted a picture of Flora Temple the fastest trotting horse in the wirld on a mahoginy buro that Pewts father is polishing for Doctor Goram Potters grandfather and i bet it will taik a weak to get it off. so i gess Pewts paist is good paist. we are going to meat at Beanys at haff past 12 oh clock. father is going to wake me at 12 oh clock. i hoap he wont forget to wake up. ennyway it wont make enny difference for i shant go to sleep. i bet we will have a good time.

Beany says it is all up with him if he dont get that dollar. he says he will be the ferst of his family to go to jale. that is what a feller gets for being in debt. Beany had augt to have wated. but i supose when a feller gets going with a girl he dont think. Beany is not bad but thinkless. i hoap it will be a lessen to him. he is feerfully wurrid but he needent be for if the wirst comes to wirst i shall sell one of my hens. i havent told him this becaus if he gnew it perhaps he wood spend the dollar for sumthing else for her. but while i have a hen to my naim Beany shall not go to jale. i wood not go to bed at all tonite if father woodent know it but if my lite aint out by 10 oh clock he hollers for me to go to bed lively. so i am going to read Grissly Ike the Scalp Lifter until 10 oh clock and then go to bed and lissen for the clock to strike 12.

September 13, 186—-this is saterday. i almost wish i was ded. i havent been out of my room sence Thursday xcept to split wood and lug water and feed the sheep and horse and hens. father says one moar sumer like this one will make a gibbering manioc of him. he says there must be sumthing rong with me. he dont know wether he had augt to lick it out of me or send me to the reform school or to a place where they keep idjuts. that is the way he talks to me but when old Decon Aspinwall and the reerent Josier Higgins and Clarisser Dorsens husband and old man Pettigrew sed i had augt to be sent to the reform school he told them to go strait to hell and try it if they thougt they cood. Beanys father has kep Beany in his room and Pewts father has kep Pewt in. the only time i can speak to Beany is after father has went to Boston and Beanys father has went down town we holler across from our chamber winders. we havent seen Pewt for his chamber is on the back of his house. i asted Beany what he was going to do about the dollar and he says he xpected the poliseman to come for him enny time. i told him if the poliseman come to tell him to come over and take the best hen i had. Beany felt better and sed i was a trew frend. he says it is a pity things is as they is but he cant help it. a feller cant help they way he feals sumtimes. peraps i am lucky that Beany has cut me out for if i had cut him out i mite be xpecting to go to jale. if i hadent heard father tell them men to go to hell i wood be afrade of going tojale or the reform school. i dont beleeve reform school or jale is enny wirse then staying in your room when a circus paraid is going by on the nex strete.

i think i will wright about what has hapened tomorrow whitch is sunday. i want to finish reading Grissly Ike the Scalp Lifter. Cele tiptode up to my room and threw it in. Cele always stands up for a feller when he is in truble. probly after the hoal thing has bloan over if it ever does Cele will tell mother she done rong in giving me the novil and will ask to be punished that is jest like Cele.

September 14, 186—-brite and fair. i am in my room wrighting. most everybody has went to chirch xcept mother who never gets time to go and father who is eether over to Pewts fathers shop or over to Beanys fathers barn talking. Beany has got his gob back becaus they found out that Pewt put the overhals and old hat into the organ. he done it to play a trick on Beany but he dident meen to lose him his gob. so it is all rite. i see Beany going to chirch. i cant go. it is tuf to have to stay in your room and not be aloud to go to chirch. that is a prety way to bring up a boy i shood say. it will be lucky for them if i dont grow up a drunkard and a robber or a berglar. some day father will be sorry for what he has did to me.

well it is a long story. last Thursday nite i fell asleep and father waked me up at 12 oh clock. i went to Beanys and found him and we went to Pewts and got the paist and the pictures. i luged one pale and Beany the other. Pewt luged the paper. we had to change hands lots of times and set the pales down. i tell you they was heavy. it was clowdy but as it was moon time it was prety lite. we dident see nobody and it seamed kind of dreery.

we got to uncle Gilmans and paisted the picture of the tapir up rite on the front side of his house. then we went to Gechels house and paisted up the giraft. we had a long handeled brush and i had to stand on Beanys shoulder to reech the girafs head. the picture reeched nearly to the roof. once we thougt we was cougt but it was only a horse kicking in the barn. we dident make enny noise and when we talked we jest wispered. it was almost as mutch fun as hooking water mellons. then we went to old Pettigrews and paisted up the boar constricter. then we went to Fatty Foggs and his dog woodent let us come near the house. we thougt he wood knaw us and Pewt hit him with a rock and he yelped so loud that old Fatty come down in his shirt tale and a little tin lamp but we was hid behine sum boards.

then we went to Clarisser Dorsens but it was all lit up and doctor Perrys horse and chase was there hiched to a poast. we wated and bimeby old man Dorson come out on the run and went down town. bimeby he came back with a old woman and they went into the house so we coodent put the stork picture on her house without being cougt and we put it on Billy Hansoms house. Billy and his wife have jest been married and last weak the fellers give them a serinaid. so we thougt they wood be pleased to be notised. by that time the town clock struck 2. so we had to hurry and them pales was heavy. so we come over the bridge and throug Clifford strete to Coart strete. Pewt he had to go into his house and while he was gone Beany sed it wood be a good goke on Pewt to put Jo Jo the Dog faced man picture on Pewts house because Pewts father has got long wiskers. so we done it and when Pewt come out we told him we had put it on old Hen Dows house and Pewt thougt that was bully.

Then Beany wanted to go in his house to get sum donuts and while he was in Pewt sed it wood be a good thing to put the Spider Monkey picture on Beanys house. Beanys father is kind of thin and wear awful tite britches and a blew coat and dresses elegant and so we done it and when Beany come out with his donuts we set down and et them and he dident notise ennything.

well after we had et the donuts we paisted up the Cheeter picture on Decon Aspinwalls house and the elefant on Horris Cobbs house and the Hineer one on the berrying yard. we tried verry hard to do a good gob there and we gnew it wood maik a fine apearance rite under the sine we are all passing away. then we come home. father let me in and asted me if i done enny damige and i sed no. he asted me where we paisted up the bills and i told him he cood see in the morning when he went to the trane. so i went to bed.

the nex morning mother come up and waked me and told me to dress and come down stairs jest as quick as i cood. she looked xcited. i asted her if ennybody was sick and she sed wirse than that. i cood hear peeple talking loud down stairs and i run down as quick as i cood get my close on and without washing my face or comeing my hair. when i got down there in the setting room i saw Billy and Mrs. Billy Hanson and old Pettigrew and Beanys father and Pewts father and the reverent Josier Higgins and old man Wiggins the trusty of the berrying ground and Decon Aspinwall and Pewt and Beany and father and mother and Aunt Sarah. and they were all piching in xcept father and mother and Aunt Sarah who dident say ennything. Mrs. Billy Hanson sed she had never been so insulted in her life. she sed she had lived a good cristian life and to have sech a insult paisted on her house was more than flesh and blud cood stand and she boohood like a big baby. and Decon Aspinwall sed he had stood all he was going to and this time the coarts wood take it up and settle it onct for all if peeple was to be insulted and defaimed and there rites trampled on and the reverent Josier sed he thougt the sacrid eddifise of whitch he was a unwerthy paster had augt to be safe from infaimus attacks and that he shood ast the coarts to rite him in the publick ey.

and old man Wiggins he sed that the ded wood tirn in there graives if they see what was on the berrying ground gait. and Beanys father sed he wasent going to be called a spider munkey for nothing and Pewts father sed he was going to find out who poasted up that Jo Jo bill befoar he left, if it took the rest of his lifetime. then they all talked together and made a feerful noise. bimeby father sed now you have all had your chance, less find out sumthing about it. so he told them what he gnew about the circus man asking us to poast the bills and Pewts father and Beanys father sed that was so. then father asted me why i done it and i told him we were told to poast the bills in apropate places to atrack attension and we done it. i sed we was going to put the stork up on Missis Dorsens house but the doctor was there and we coodent and so we put it on Misses Hansons. and then Missis Hanson saled into me like time again then Pewts father sed Pewt sed he dident know ennything about puting the Jo Jo bill on his house and i sed he was in the house then and Beanys father sed Beany sed he dident know about the spider munkey bill and i sed Beany was in the house then and i done it.

then they all sed i was the ring leeder and had led Pewt and Beany into temptasion and old Decon Aspinwall sed it was mity queer that we dident put up ennything on fathers house and the boy was the father of the man and that he wood see that i was sent to the reform school and that father paid heavy damages.

that was the time father got mad and told him to go to hell and old Decon went off to see his lawyer. then father told the others that he wood do all he cood to make it rite and he took me round to all of them to their houses and made me beg their pardon. peeple were scraping the pictures off and washing them with hot water and evrybody was laffing.

Uncle Gilman and Mister Gechel and Horris Cobb all laffed and sed it was a good goke but the others were all feerful mad with me and father and not very mad with Pewt and Beany. that is all rite but the idea of me leading Pewt and Beany into temtasion makes me sick.

well Pewt got a licking and Beany got a licking and i got a licking and we have all got to stay in the house until school begins. but Beany had to go to chirch to keep his gob.

it is prety tuf to stay in a fellers room and to hear a circus band playing and not go jest becaus we tride to do the best we cood. ennyway i am glad i aint going to the reform school. father jest come in with a paper. he sed he had been arested and had to get bale. he sed old Decon Aspinwall had sewed him for 10 thousand dollars for defaiming his caracter. father sed old Decon had to go to Portsmouth for a lawyer, and that Amos Tuck and General Marstin and Judg Stickney and Alvy Wood all come up and sed they wood see him throug without paying a dam cent. father feals prety good tonite. Aunt Sarah says he always does when there is a chane for a fite.

this is the ferst time in my life i ever hoaped school wood begin. ennything is beter than staying in your room.

September 15, 186—-school begun today and i went. i dident supose i ever wood ruther go to school than stay in my room espeshully a school whitch is taugt by old Francis. but they is always sumthing lively taiking place in old Francis school. sumtimes Micky Guold is setting down on tacts or the points of pens whitch has been stuck in his seet so they wont fall over like a bent pin whitch aint mutch good enyway most of the time and hollering bludy merder and geting snached baldheaded for it by old Francis, or Beany or Bug Chadwick is being ferriled with a hard wood ruler with 2 hairs in the pam of there hand to splitt the old ruler into fraggments whitch i have never seen did yet in this life or licked sumwhere else whare nuthing will do enny good xcept a peace of paistboard or the Exeter Newsleter in the set of their britches, or Pop Clark is maid to eat a apple before the hoal school as fast as he can with rot and wirm holes and wirms and the stem and seeds and the coar or Skinny Bruce is being snaiked over 2 seets and put in the woodbox with the cuvver down because Gim Erly whitch sits behine Skinny put a pin in the toe of his shue and reeched over and kicked Tady Finton whitch sits in front of Skinny and old Francis wont believe Skinny but licks him onct for doing it and twict for liing about it whitch he says is twict as wirse as doing it, or Fatty Gilman is down on all foars and howling while old Francis lams him with the haff of the broom stick he stirs the fire with while Fatty is triing hard to crawl throug a chair whitch he cant do enny moar than the cammel cood crawl throug the ey of the needle in the bible.

All of them things is taiking place in old Francis school every day whitch makes it a very intersting place when you are not the feller whitch is doing them things but is setting down and waching them out of the coner of your ey and pertending to studdy hard whitch nobudy can do when sumbuddy is howling terruble and banging agenst seets and you never know when your tern wil come nex.

but it is lots beter than staying in your room and not seing the fellers and coppying there xamples and getting so far behine in your studdies that you are shoar to get licked evry day for a week or 2. there is sum fun in geting licked onct in a while if you have a chance to escaip and it is a grate deel moar fun if sumbuddy else gets licked for sumthing you have did. sumtimes a feller will tel on sumbuddy else and then evry feler whitch can lick him licks him the ferst time they gets the chance. but most of the fellers will take another fellers lickings without a yip. Old Francis lickings is wirse than 2 or 3 of another fellers lickings but aint so bad as 30 or 40 lickings whitch a feller is shoar to get if he tells on anuther feller to say nuthing about the girls running their tungs out at you and calling you tattle tail and stiking their nose up in the air when they goes by you whitch maiks a feller feal prety cheep whitch is sumtimes wirse than a licking.

So on the hoal i had ruther go to school than stay in my room whitch dont make enny diference becaus i have got to go ennyway wether i want to or not.

tonite i had to studdy Colburn arithmatic. it is the wirst book i ever studded. i bet there aint a boy in this wirld whitch doesnt want to paist time out of old Colburn. i had ruther be a merderer if nomuddy gnew it than be a feler whitch rote a arithmatic. Ennyway old Colburn had a key whitch tells jest how to do the xamples and has them all figgered out. teechers is aloud to have the key but the scholers cant have it. Enny time old Francis dont know how to do a xample he looks in his key and lerns how and then a feller whitch dont have a key is snached baldheaded becaus he dont know how to do it. i dont think that is fair. i had 10 xamples to do and i have got them all did. Cele done 4 and Keene 3 and father 3. so i am all rite tomorrow. father give me 2 bats in the ear befoar i undestood one xample. Keene gets mad but she dont dass to bat me. Cele is the best.

September 16, 186—-brite and fair. i havent let my boat for a long time. Pewts' father has got the best boats now. it was prety quite in school today only 9 fellers got licked. five of them hollered to make old Francis stop. Scotty Briggim never hollers and Stubby Gooch and Tady Tilton and Jack Mevlin dont ever holler. Nigger Bell never got but one licking and he hollered louder than enny feller i ever herd Old Francis dont lick him becaus he hollers so loud.

September 17, 186—-brite and fair. i havent had a cent for moar than a weak. it is tuf to be so poar. i have got to rase sum chink sumhow. Beany aint paid me my 40 cents yet.

September 18, 186—-i got licked today in school. jest for nothing. sum one put sum gum in Medo Thirstems seet and he coodent get up to resite and old Francis yanked him up and found the gum and licked me becaus i set jest behine his seet. he sed he had been keeping his ey on me for a long time. it cant be very long becaus school has only been 3 days. today was wensday and there wasent enny school in the afternoon. me and Putter went up river fishing and caught 8 pickeril. prety good for us.

September 19, 186—-brite and fair. nex weak is the county fair and cattle show. i am going. the band is pracktising evry nite and that is the reeson i cant get my lessons. no feller can studdy when a band is playing king John quickstep and red stocking quickstep and romanse from Leeclare and departed days and things like them rite across the strete. so i miss in my lessons and get licked most every day. sum day i am going to play in a band. i shall play a e flat cornet like old Robinson and Bruce Briggim and Rashe Belnap. they played a new peace tonite. i shoodent think men whitch cood play in a band wood ever do ennything else. i never wood.

September 20, 186—-rany as time. i hoap it wont rane next weak when they are having the fare. tonite it raned so hard that the band dident pracktise so i had time to studdy. i coodent do ennything this afternoon but set in Ed Toles barn and see the horses rubed down.

September 21, 186—-brite and fair today. i went to chirch today. After chirch me and father went up to the fair grounds. they have got a lot of sheds bilt and most of the fence is up and the ralings round the track. i bet it will be a good fair.

Peekily Tiltons father plays in the band and 3 uncles. his father plays a b flat tenner horn and his uncle Ed plays a e flat base horn and his uncle George plays an e flat alto horn and his uncle Warrin plays a b flat cornet. Peeliky says he is going to play some day. he doesnt know what he will play but he wil play sumthing. i asted father why he dident play in the band and he sed they was dam fools enuf in the wirld without he being one. i was going to ast him to by me a cornet but i desided i woodent jest yet. i gnew jest what he wood say if i asted him.

father says he dont like band playing but i notise he stays to home the nites the band plays and sets on the steps an lisens and beets time with his foot and sumtimes puts in as good base as Ed Tilton, Peeliky Tiltons uncle can with his base horn and when sumbuddy in the band plays out of tune he gumps up and waulks up and down the piaza and says why dont they hit that feller with a ax. so i know he likes band playing as wel as i do. i wish he played in the band fer then i wood go into the bandroom and hear them. me and Beany tride to go in one nite and we was jest going up stairs when sumbuddy throwed a hoal pale of water on us and we skined out pretly lifely. i woodent care if they only wood let us in after they had throwed the water but they hollered get out of here you little devils or we will drownd you. i bet them band fellers can lick enny other band fellers and beat them playing two. i bet our band is as good as enny band in the wirld.

September 22, 186—-i am terible xcited. we are going to have three days vacasion this week while they have the fair and cattle show and i have got a seeson ticket becaus Charles Talor is going to have Nellie to drive the hoal time. he gets the hay and grane and straw for the annimals and has got to be going in and out of the fair grounds al the time and father has let him have Nellie and he give me and father a seeson tickit. so i kin go all the time so long as i split my kinlins and get in my wood and all the pales of water mother wants. Beanys father is going to ride in percession as marchal with a yeller sash on and long yeller gloves on and a stick with red and white and blew ribbons on it and so Beany has got a seeson tickit two and Pewts father is going to put sum golden pollish hens and sum rocky mountain hens in the hen show and so Pewt has got a seeson ticket. Beany has pade me back my forty cents. i tell you there aint many fellers whitch has as good luck as i have got. 3 days vacasion and a season tickit to a fair and cattle show and plenty of money. i dont se what else a feller cood want. tonite i studded as hard as i cood with a band playing 2 or 3 new peaces. Cele helped me with my examples. it wont do for me to miss in my lessons tomorrow or nex day. i gess with Celes help i can hang on for 2 days more after that i dont care so mutch.

September 32, 186—-it looks like rane. i hoap it wil rane today if it ranes this weak. today i saw a man drive throug town in a high wheal gig hiched to a auful long legged horse. the man had on a cap with a long viser and had pullers on his ranes and had 2 pales hung under his gig and set on a lot of blankits and the horse had on a white blanket with red letters on it whitch sed Flying Tiger 2.57 enterd for the free for all. he asted Tommy Tomson the way to the fair grounds and Tommy sed he cood show him and he clim into the gig and drove off. well Tommy he staid to the fair grounds all the forenoon and in the afternon old Francis licked him and made him holler two but Tommy sed it was worth it to stay to the fair grounds haff a day and get out of school for one licking. he sed it dident hurt mutch and he only hollered to make him stop. Tommy says they have bilt a bandstand and a stand for the juges and pens for the pigs and hens and cattle and resterants and pop corn places and evrything else. i wood like to go up tonite but father says i cant go up until the ferst day of the fair.

Tommy says there is going to be a snaik charmer and a bull whitch gives milk and a girl whitch has got 2 heads and 4 legs and 4 arms and a sheep with 6 legs. mother says i cant go in to see the girl with 4 legs becaus its impropper to look at a girls legs. i asted father and he sed it is twict as impropper to look at a 4 leged girls legs as a 2 leged one so i cant go in to see that.

Tommy sed they was going to be a troting race for bulls. Charley Treadwill has got a big white and black bull named Nickerbocker whitch he drives in a wagon with a bit in his mouth and he is going to have a race with a bull from Portsmouth. i bet on Charleys bull. i wish it was a bull fite. i wood bet on Charleys bull.

old Wakeup Robinson is going to trot his horse Prince John. they is going to have 2 bands the Exeter band and the Newmarket band. i bet the Exeter band is the best. i cant hardly wate for tomorrow.

i dident miss in school today and tonite we set out on the steps to hear the band. old wisler Weeks is going to play a fife in the band and old Potsy Dirgin is going to play a fife two.

September 24, 186—-brite and fair and county fair two. that is a goke and a good one two but nobuddy will ever see it but me. gosh i am tired tonite i never had so much fun in my life. we had the best percession i ever see. first come the marchals George Perkins and John Gardner and Beanys father and old Francis and John Gibson all on white horses xcept George Perkins and John Gardner and old Francis whitch was on red horses and Jon Gibson whitch was on a spoted horse and they all looked fine. then come the Exeter band and then a lot of ox teems full of wimen in white with their hides all brushed up with curry combs and their horns all cuvered with ribbons and evergreens in their slats. i tell you when old Giddings and old Wiliam Conner and old Nat Gilman jabbed them with the ox godes they walked along prety lifely. then come the Newmarket band and then the fire ingine and a lot of men with cains and stove pipe hats and then a steam wagon and then Charles Tredwill driving his bull and old wakeup Robinson with his troter and a sope pedler with a humpback horse. it was the best percession i ever see. the Exeter band played 4 times as loud as the Newmarket band. i wish you cood have heard Peeliky Tiltons uncles play you wood have thougt they wood bust their cheeks but they dident. Fatty Walker broak 2 heads on his base drum the ferst day and Len Heirvey broak one in the snair drum. I gnew they wood beat the Newmarket band. tonite father and mother and Cele and Keene and Georgie have went to the haughticulture show in the town hall. they have all sorts of frutes and beens and pees and beets and flowers and gars of frute and perserves and bread and cake and pyes to see whitch has maid the best and gnitting and sowing things and drawings and paintings and bea hives and stufed birds and a stufed wilcat showing her teeth. it is ded so it cant hirt ennybuddy and composisons of school girls and handwriting and lots of things. i wanted to go but father sed i codent go to evrything. i gess i will go to bed. i have got a verry bizy day tomorow. Beany is going to try and get a gob tomorow.

September 25, 186—-brite and fair again. i am prety tired again tonite and am staying to home. father and arnt Sahar and Keene and Cele and Georgie have went to the haughticulchure show this time and me and mother are staying to home. mother is rocking the baby and i am in my room wrighting. today there was a percession this morning and i was in it but only a litle while. i held one end of the base drum but evry time Fatty Walker wood hit it a good belt he wood send me flying round sideways and at the end of the ferst peace i felt jest as if old Francis had shook my livver out. so i give it up. so they got Curley Conner a big feller. Fatty cood bang the drum as hard as he cood lam it but he coodent nock Curley round.

today the Exeter band beat the Newmarket band again. it scart 4 horses and made them run awa and smashed 3 wagons and throwed out 14 people and the Newmarket band only scart one horse and dident throw out enny peeple. i tell you Exeter can beat Newmarket evry time.

Me and Pewt and Beany all got a chance to take a gob. the man that hollers for Julia the snaik charmer offerd us 1 doller apeace if we wood stand up on the platform and let a boar constricter coil around us and then Julia the snaik charmer wood come out and charm the snaiks and save our lifes. you bet we dident take that gob.

Beany got a gob hollering for a peap show of war pictures but his father come riding up and snaiked him out. i give 5 cents of my 40 cents that Beany pade me to get a shock in a lectric machine and when i got hold of the handels i coodent let go. i felt like a crasy boan

79

all over and i danced and hollered till Jerry Carter come up and told the man if he dident stop the machine he wood smash it and smash him two so the man he stopped it and i let go and run. Everybuddy laffed but me and Jerry Carter.

then we went to the track to see the bull race. there was a big black bull hiched into a gig troting up and down the track and they were wating for Charly Tredwill and Nickerbocker. bimeby he come troting down the track and when the red bull see the other he stopd and pawed the ground and bellered and Nickerboker he done the sam and both men begun to lick them but the bulls dident notise it enny more than if a fli stang them and they put their heds down and began to push and butt and hook and roar and they tiped over the gig and the wagon and throwed Charly and the other man out and stepped on Charly Tredwill's head and nocked down the rales and went bang agenst the Juges stand and everybuddy hollered for Charlys bull xcept about haff of them whitch hollered for the other bull but nobuddy dassed to go near them. bimeby the Captain of the Ingine company whitch was going to have a xibition squirt hollered to the fellers to start the breaks and they done it and begun to squert rite on the bulls heads and they coodent stand it and they stoped fiting. they were all tuckered out and there harnasses and wagons was all smashed to kinlin wood. it was beter than enny dog fite i ever see. every buddy sed it was the best thing in the show. i wish they had let them fite it out. i bet Charlys bull wood lick. father sed twict that Charly wasent hirt becaus his head was solid way through. that enny feller whitch wood fool away his time to trane a bull to trot in a race coodent be hirt by ennything stepping on his head. Beany has got a gob as waiter in a resterrent. he got 50 cents yesterday. Pewt got 50 cents in working for a feler whitch has a lot of poasts and a lot of rings. the poasts is all numbered and they is a preasent for every poast. You give 10 cents to toss a ring. if you toss it good and it goes over a poast you get a gold wach or a 12 blaided gnife or a gold headed cain or a sigar or a whip or a doll or a glass pitcher. i tossed it over a poast and got a sigar and i give the sigar to old Barny Casidy and he lit it and took 2 puffs and spit it out and sed it was made of a old horse blanket. tomorrow is the last day of the fair and if i am going to ern enny money i have got to get a gob pretty quick. father is going to stay at home tomorow to go to the fair. i have had a auful good time today and seen some good races but i havent had a gob. Pewt and Beany always have the luck.

September 28, 186—-this is a rany sunday. i cant go to chirch becaus my paint has not come off yet. i shood not dass to go to chirch becaus peeple wood laff rite out loud. father says he dont believe it will ever come off. but mother says it will with plenty of greece and soft sope. i am most raw now. i wish father had kiled that man. i never got into so bad a scraip before. father says that he has desided that the reform school or the idjut assilem is the only place for me but mother says i needent wurry about that for that is only his talk but i must be more cairful in the future. i told her i dident meen ennything rong but only wanted to earn a little money and she sed she gnew that but there is sum ways of erning money whitch is open to objecsion and i gess she is rite and this is one of them ways. After a feller has had his skin scrubed with soft sope and bristol brick for two days jest like pollishing a brass door gnocker he wishes he was ded.

Well you see i maid up my mind to get a gob becaus Beany had and Pewt had and i had spent all my money. so the first thing i done when i had did my choars was to put for the fair grounds erly. when i got there i went to the resterrent and asted them if they wanted a waiter. they sed no but they was a feller whitch had a tent nex to Julia the snaik charmer whitch has ben triing to get 2 boys. so i went over there and there was a new tent and a big picture painted on a sheet of the wild men of Bornio whitch was captured after a dredful fite in whitch 6 bludhounds was kiled and 4 men fataly injered for life. they was a picture of soldiers and hunters with guns and bludhounds chasing the 2 wild men and carring off the wounded men and the ded dogs.

when i got there i saw a big man with a big mustash talking with Hiram Mingo a nigger boy. i asted him if he had a gob for me and he looked at me and sed i was pretty skinny but perhaps he cood fix me. he asted us into the tent. i woodent go for i was afrade of the wild men of Bornio but he sed the tent was emty. so we went in and he sed he had bad luck. That both his wild men was sick and he had a wife and nine small children, and he had got to earn there bread and the only way to do it was to get sum kind hearted feller like us to be wild men. he sed if we wood do that for him he wood pay us 2 dollars apeace and his nine children and his sick wife and blind mother wood pray for us on her gnees. i was auful sorry for him he looked so sad. he sed he had looked up a lot of feller and talked with a lot and we was the only fellers that was smart enuf to do it. he sed he never was gnew to maik a mistake in a feller. he gnew he cood trust us enny time. so i asted him what we wood have to do and he sed he wood paint us up like wild men and put on sum firs and leperd skins and sum brass rings on our hine legs and a necklace of tiger claws and all we wood have to do was to snarl and say yowk and let out howls, and try to get at peeple. i dident want to black up but Hiram dident care becaus he is a nigger. so is asted him if the black wood ware off and he sed yes and so after a while i sed i wood. well he made me take off all my close and he painted me all over black and he put sum black stuf on my hair and twisted out all the points whitch stuck up, then he wound a leperd skin round me and round Hiram and i had a neck lace of tiger claws and 2 brass rings round my hine legs. then he took sum red paint and he painted sum big scars on us where tigers had toar us. when he showed me in the looking glass how it looked it scart me. i never would have gnew it was me. i was wirse looking than a babboon.

then he learned us how to snarl and yowl and make faces. he sed it was easier for me to make faces than enny feller he had ever gnew and he sed it must come natural to me. He sed i wood scare a gorilla white. then he lerned us how to fite and sed we must snarl and fite when he was out on the platform telling the peeple about us and then we wood rush in and crack a whip and fire a pistol in our faces and stop us.

Well after we had lerned how he put a ox chane on to us and then he went out and begun to holler. he sed ladies and gentlemen for one short day only you are privileged to see the wild men of Bornio, imported at vast expense by arrangements with the king of Bornio and captured after a terific fite after 6 dogs was killed and 4 men fataly ingered for life. they are of small size but like the man munky they have the strength of 7 strong men in their sinews and boans and in there native lair they track and kill the maneeting tiger and the lion with there naked hands. then he pounded his stick twict on the platform and it was a signal to us and we begun to yowl and snarl and stamp and he sed there they are taring each other to bits and he rushed in and hollered and cracked his whip and fired his pistal and we yowled and snarld and peeple begun to rush up and pay 10 cents to come in. when they saw us one woman sed my what dredful looking things and one man sed i have got a 15 years old boy that can lick boath of them munkys. so when he and his boy come near the platform i gumped at him and made a auful face and let out a auful howl and i wish you cood have seen that 15 years old boy hiper acrost that tent and holler. he was scart most to deth and the man two and a woman screached and they had to carry her out. then the man cracked his whip and drove me back snarling and making auful faces and Hiram he let out sum auful yowls and bit his chane and fomed at the mouth with sope and the man told how only last weak he had to put on us a red hot iron to drive us off a hieener whitch had got out of its cage and had atacted us but he was two lait and before he cood drive us from our pray we toar him to bits.

A man asted what we et and he sed live rabits and chickings and sometimes frogs. well peeple kep coming in droves and bimeby i see Beany an Pewt come. Beanys eyes were jest like sorcers. i laid down and snarled a litle and i pertended to be asleep and snarled in my sleep like a dog does. i wanted Beany to come near me and so i kep quite and bimeby Beany and Pewt come close to the platform and i make a gump at them and let out the loudest yowl and maid the feerfullst face i cood.

wel Beany went heels over head and hollered bludy merder and Pewt he div rite out under the bottom of the tent and that is the last i see of them. a lot of people come in whitch i gnew and i scart a lot of them most to deth and old mister Emerson lost his false teeth and dident das to come back after them. i never had so mutch fun in my life. bimeby i see father and Charles Talor come in. when they see us Talor begun to laff and sed thunder George the skinny munky faced one is skinny enuf to be your boy and father laffed and sed did you ever see sutch a looking thing in your life. i wated till they come up and then i gumped to the end of my chane and yowled feerful and toar my hair and stamped my feet and made faces and snarled auful and Hiram done the same. they kep back out of reech and father sed well if them is the kind of things fellers see whitch has the delirim tremens i never shall taik another drink what do you say Talor and they laffed and went out. well we scart peeple all that day and had a grate time. at dinner he closed the tent and give us sumthing to eat and drink and then in the afternoon we done the same thing. we got prety tired of it but we kep on. bimeby father come in again and looked round and asted sum men if they had seen his boy. they sed no and he went away. bimeby he come in agen and stood and looked at us a long time. i was tired and dident yowl so mutch. after awhile he come up near and i made a gump at him and knashed my teeth. he kep back so i coodent tare him whitch was a good thing for him for he wood have broak my back and he sed that is the ferst time i ever see blew eyd nigger and he kept looking. well a lot of peeple come in and the man begun to talk about us and pounded the

platform and we had augt to have fit, but we was boath prety sick of
it and he cracked his whip clost to Hiram and snached a peace of
skin off his back and it hirt Hiram so bad that he forgot he was a
wild man of Bornio and had been toar by a tiger and he begun to ball
and in a minit evrybuddy was hollering cheet cheet and father
jumped over the raling and grabed me and yanked me off that
platform and men were hollering kill the cheet and evrybuddy was
trying to get at him and codent find him for he had got out sumway.
wel father sed you infernal idjut where is your close and i sed in that
trunk and he opened the trunk and got out my close and made me
put them on and Hiram he put his on and peeple were hollering for
there money back for it was a cheet and i sed where is my 2 dollars
and father sed what you ned is 2 lickings and that is what you will
get when i get you home if i can ever get your hide clean enuf to lick
and he got Charles Talor to drive up with Nellie and took me home.
When we come out of the tent they was a big crowd whitch holllered
and laffed at us and all the fellers hollered Plupy the niger munky
and Plupy the wild man of Bornio. it was tuf on me for all Hiram
Mingo had to do was to put on his close and hat and he was all rite.
well when we got home and went into the house mother was so
surprised that she nerly dropped the baby. i gess she wood have but
he begun to howl and grab her round the neck and hold his breth
and grow black in the face and Franky and Annie howled and held
on to her skerts and to aunt Sarahs two and they had to be took out
of the room and when mother and aunt Sarah come back they sed
what have you got there George and father sed it is your smart son,
and mother sed what has he been doing now, and father sed he has
been a wild man of Bornio at 10 cents a whack and mother and arnt
Sarah sed well of all things in this wirld and then they begun to laff
until the teers roled down there cheaks and father sed i know it aint
no laffing matter and mother sed i know it aint and then she lafed so
it hirt her side. bimeby father sed what are we going to do. i draw
the line at bringing up a babboon or a man munky in this family.

So mother and aunt Sarah and father and me went down to the
kitchen and got a tub and filled it with warm water and they put me
in and then they scrubed me with soft sope and then they took me
out and most of the black was on. the water was sum black but they
sed they coodent see it was enny blacker than when i took my reglar
Saterday bath. then they filled the tub again and scrubed me with
soft sope and bristol brick. it about skined me and maid me holler.
that took off sum of the black. then they tride seesand and that hirt
so they had to stop so they greesed me with lard and wiped it off

84

and father sed i was improving. he sed i looked like a half nigger and he guessed nex week they cood get me to look like a quarune and praps weak after nex like a octerune.

i have got to stay in until i get white again. mother says i am the wirst looking thing she ever see in her life. father is talking about reform school again but i ges i needent wurry. today i was two soar to be scrubed so i was greased and wiped off.

Tomorrow if i am not two soar they are going to try bristol brick and soft soap again. i had my head shaived. father done it with the horse clippers. tomorrow if i am not two soar they are going to try bristol brick and soft sope again i asted father if they cougt that man and he sed no they never wood. it is tuf to end a weak this way. it is a auful xperience for a feller whitch has always tride to do rite.

September 29, 186—-today they almost skined me alive. i feel like a haol pimpel all red and swole up. after they get throug skining me with soft sope and bristol brick and seesand they greece me all over. they are using mutten taller now becaus lard is too xpensive so mother says, and father says it suits me for i am the champeen mutten hed. i ges i am a quadrune now. it taiks me a hoal day to get over being skun so they can skin me again. i asted father why he coodent put me in a tirning laith and tirn me down jest like they maik wheal hubs down to old Gus Browns hub shop. father he sed it looked as if he wood have to and he wood see Gus about it today. ennyway i dont beleeve it wood hirt as mutch as seesand.

September 30, 186—-Beany come in to see me today. he laffed so that i told him if he dident stop i wood give him a bang in the snoot so he stoped. we plade checkers and dominose. he can beet me evry time. Beany says i cant go in swiming enny more for 4 years becaus if i get wet the black comes back. gosh i wunder if that is so. i have been reeding Uncle Toms Cabbin and i dont like it enny moar. i asted mother if what Beany sed was trew and she laffed and sed of coarse it aint in your blud and i sed it wood get in if they wasent prety cairful not to scrub me two hard.

i asted father about it when he come home and he sed he wasent sure. he sed it depended sum on how i behaved. that sumtimes a feller wood tirn black with raige, and if he had been blacked up it mite come back. i told him i wood do the best i cood if i ever got white again. i asted how he suposed i ever was fool enuf to do what i had did and he sed it seamed to be eesier for me to be a fool than for most folks. then he sed i was too anchious for money. he sed it reminded him of a line in a poim whitch was rote by a lattin gentleman naimed Publius virgin. i asted him if he was enny relasion of old John Virgin whitch oaned the trotting horses and he sed no he dident think he cood be. if he was it must be straned prety fine. the line went like this

    a cused thirst for gold to what dust
    thou compel the human mind

i rote it down jest as father sed it. i dont know what it means but i dident dass to tel him that and so i sed yes sir i woodent be surprised if it done jest that.

I wish i cood go to school again. i wood be willing to have old Francis lam me.

i suppose the fellers will all laff and call me munkey face and wild man of Bornio but i woodent cair for that. tomorrow i shall be well enuf to be scrubed again. tonite i am greeced and almost too slipery to lay in bed. i am glad i am not a eal or a hornpout. i feel jest like them only i aint got enny horns.

September 31. brite and fair. i have been scrubed again. i bet they was sum fishooks in that seesand. it felt so. enyway i am a octerune now and most white. mother says one moar greecing will be enuf.

September 32, 186—-the last time i was greeced i had the itch. it wasent as bad as this but i remember it well.

September 33 186—-today i went down town. i have been away a long time but the town looks about the saim. Kelley and Gardners have sole 2 gnifes and Fogg and Fellows have sole sum pipes and a cuppy Olliver Optics magazene and old Luke Langly has sole a gointed comb and a tin horn and wagon but in other respecks things look about the saim. i am glad i wasent away long enuf for the place to chainge. that wood be dreadful. i herd of a man onct whitch was sent to jale for his hoal life. bimby they was a new king in the land and he let out the men whitch was in jale this poar man was so glad to get out that he run 9 miles all the way home but when he got home evrything had chainged. where his house was stood a methydist chapel and where his frends house was they had bilt a pest house for small pocks pashients and where the green house stood they had bilt a glue factory and where the libary stood they was a slauter house. but in spite of all these improovments he did not feal to home and he was verry loansum. so he went back to the king and gnelt down on his gnees and sed nobble and venial monnark send me back to jale for my friends are scatered and my house is gone. so the king whitch was a verry kind harted monnark sent him back to jale where he lived hapily many years on bread and water and sumtimes only water.

so i know jest how he felt when i come down town the ferst time to see if things had chainged. but they havent mutch.

September 34, 186—-well of all the big fools i ever see in my life they aint no September 31 or 32 or 34 and i rote them down. this is

87

October 4. there was a frost last nite. i wanted to go to school this morning but mother sed i had beter wait until Monday and begin fresh. so i done errants and split wood and luged pales of water and raiked leeves this afternoon and me and Potter rew up the river to the rapids. the lily pads was all ded and the leeves of the trees was red and yellow. the blewgays was calling and it semed kind of loansume. it seamed good to row again in a boat. tomorrow i shall go to chirch. i have missed chirch a good deel. i never thougt i cood. i never thougt i cood miss school but i have.

October 5, 186—-i went to chirch today. the minister preeched about our duty to our father and mother. i have been thinking a grate deel laitly about how litle i have amounted to and what a lot of truble i have gave my parents and my frens. when a feller is kep in his room prety near all summer suffering from a awful soar skin diseeze caused by being painted black by a man whitch had augt to have gnew better and scrubed with soft sope and bristol brick and seesand to get off the black and not knowing from day to day and from weak to weak wether he will be a nigger or a white man all the rest of his life i tell you he begins to think over the mean things he has did and resolv to do better if he ever gets well and has the chanct. and when a feller gets well and gets a chanct as i have did he aint mutch of a feler if he brakes his resolvs and hadent augt to get well.

father has always gave me a good edjucasien and i have lerned to read well and to spel acuraitly and the multiplacsion table is rite at the end of my tung and i can wright down enny table without looking in the book. the hardest is 9 but it is jest as easy to me as 1.

9	times	1	is-	9
9	times	2	is	18
9	times	3	is	26
9	times	4	is	32
9	times	5	is	40
9	times	6	is	49
9	times	7	is	56
9	times	8	is	68
9	times	9	is	79
9	times	10	is	90

there if eny feller can do enny better than that i shood like to see him. then i can bound New Hampshire and i know all the counties in the state whitch will be of the gratest asistence to me when i go out into the wirld to maik my fortune. i only wish father had a morgige on his home but he hasent. if he had i wood come back sum time to pay it. i asted father one day why he dident have a mortgige and he sed he dident have enny home to morgige but had to hire a house of J. Albert Clark. father sed that enny feller with 40 leven children to suport whitch cood by him a house or a farm was smarter than he was.

so i have desided first to give up Beany and Pewt. it will be tuf to give them up. peeple sumtimes have to strugle hard to give up smoaking and drinking but sumtimes they doesent. Pwets father and Beanys father will be glad beaus they boath says that neither Pewt or Beany ever done a rong thing befoar they were so frendly with me. so i am glad there will be sumone whitch will be glad of it. ennyway i gess they dont know Pewt and Beany so well as i do. i cood tell sum things about them if i was meen enuf. i talked it over with Cele and she thinks if i wood reed the palsams evry day it wood help but i am afrade i coodent do boath. i wunder if pewt and Beany can get along without me. i hoap they will be able to stand it but i woodent be surprised if they coodent without sum suffering.

ennyway they have got to stand it becaus from this time we aint going together enny moar. of coarse i shall speek to them when i meat them and say hi Beany and hi Pewt but they wont be enny moar ringing door bells nites and plugging tomatose and grean apples. that will be hard two because it is jest the time for them things and the cucumbers is brite yeller and full of guice and seeds. if a feller waring a stove pipe hat shood come along the strete when i was near a tomatoe vine or a cucumber bush i am afraide i shood have to let ding at him. i dont beleeve the palsams wood do enny good. there is sum things that no feller can stand. but i am going to do the best i can even if i am like a solitary sandpiper or hork whitch always goes aloan. i am not going to tell the folks jest what i am going to do. they will find out later by my acks. sum fellers talks two mutch. i am not goin to be 1 of that kind. i am going to keep my mouth shet and do rite and no feller can do rite if he goes round with Pewt and Beany and fellers like them. i like them boath better than i like the best scolars in school and the fellers whitch dont never miss in there lessons but a feller has got to do his duty sum times in his life. i am going to bed and try to sleap but i dont beleeve i shall sleap a winck.

October 6, 186—-brite and fair. i went to school today for the ferst time. the fellers was glad to see me. they augt to have been becaus they maid lots of fun of me. they call me the wild man of Bornio and munkey face and scrached themselves and pertended to be awful soar. but i dident cair i was so glad to get back to school and to see the fellers that they cood hav called me ennything. ennyway a feller whitch has been called polelegs and skinny and daddy long legs and yeller legs dont mind a few moar nicnaims. i dident get licked today but ame pretty near getting. it seamed like old times to set at my desk and see old Francis shake the fellers up. old Francis aint changed a bit.

tonite i was raiking up leeves when Beany come over. i sed hi Beany and he ses hi Plupy. what are you doing raiking leeves and i sed yes. he sed have you got anuther raik and i sed no. then he sed when you get tired i will raik and i sed aint going to get tired. then he sed if you aint it will be the ferst time. then i sed peraps and i kep on raiking. then he sed i have got a raik to home and i will go over and get it and come back and help you i sed you needent truble yourself. and he sed it is more fun wirking then setting round doing nuthing and i sed that is why i am wirking. then he sed well i will get my raik and i sed if you have got enny raiking to do you can do it in your own yard and Beany he stopd and looked at me sirprised and sed what is eeting of you Plupy and i sed nuthing is eeting of me, and he sed what have i did and i sed nuthing and Beany he sed what maiks you ack so queer and i sed i aint acking queer and he sed you are two and i sed i aint neetner and he sed sumthing is certainly eeting of you and i sed no there aint nothing eeting of me only this is my gob and i am going to do it without enny help. then Beany he sed all rite Plupy if that is the way you are going to ack i bet it is the last time i ever offer to help you and i sed i hoap so and Beany he went off wisling loud without maiking enny tune.

i set out to call him back and maik up with him but i dident. i kep on raiking and looked at Beany out of the corner of my ey but he dident look back and he was waulking stif leged and when Beany waulks that way you mite jest as well give up. he is as obstinite as a mule.

after supper i finished raiking and then split up my kinlins. after i had split them i forgot and started for Beanys but jest as i was going out of my yard i remembered that me and Beany was throug. so i went back and set on the steps. Beany Pewt and Medo Thirston and Nipper and sum of the other fellers was playing club the gool and the gool was in Beanys yard so i coodent go out and play becaus me and Beany was throug. i was crasy to play but i coodent. after dark i studded hard but i coodent lern ennything becaus i cood hear Beany and the other fellers hollering and laffing. i bet Beany done it a perpose. enyway Beany you jest wate till tomorrow and and see what you will get when old Francis finds out you havent studded your leson, and you two Pewt.

October 7, 186—-went to school today. Beany dident speek to me. so i wated till he got his licking for not having his lesson. well you never see sutch luck as Beany has. they was jest 1 xample i hadent done. Cele coodent do it or Keene and father had went down town. so i thougt i woodent be called up on that sum. wel i got called up on that sum and coodent do it and got licked and Beany got called up after i had missed and i thougt it wood be sum fun to see Beany licked. well what do you think Beany he up and done the example rite. i never was so sirprised in my life. then old Francis told me i had augt to be ashaimed of myself. that if i had did as Elbrige, Elbrige is Beany you know, done and staid in and studded insted of romeing the stretes i woodent have missed. i sed yes sir. i wood like to know how Beany done that xample. i saw Pewt today and spoke to him. he acted queer. i wonder if Beany told him.

tonite the fellers plaid again in Beanys yard. they plaid coram. most always they play coram in the school yard where there is moar room but tonite they plaid it in Beanys yard. so i coodent do ennything but set on the steps after i had done my choars. they aint much fun in that. i miss Beany a good deel. it is going to be hard to keep away from him but it is the rite thing to do. it is 2 days that i havent got in enny scraip. if i had been going with Beany and Pewt i wood have got in some scraip befoar this. it is 2 days sence i have had enny fun. but it shall get used to it after a while. i studded hard tonite with Cele and Keene and got all my xamples. Keene says i dont try. it aint enny of her bisiness. she only done two of them and Cele the other 8.

but i notise that the ones whitch does the leest has the most to say. if Keene says mutch more about me i wont let her do enny moar of my xamples. so she had better be cairful what she says. i am going to bed erly for they aint enny of the fellers to talk to.

October 8, 186—-brite and fair. i went to school today. dident miss in my lessons mutch not enuf to get licked. Beany had sum good luck and sum how he did his xample rite. Pewt missed but xplained the reeson so well that he dident even get shook. Pewt is grate fer that. he can ast questions so as to maik old Francis think he knows sumthing about it when he dont know ennything. i wish i cood do that. if i dont know the xample i cant ack as if i did, i am wateing for Beany to get a good licking to pay him for being meen to me nites and having all the fellers play in his yard. i bet i woodent have did that to him.

this afternoon there wasent enny school and i thougt i wood have sum fun. i went down to Ed Toles but he had went to drive a man to North Kamton. Frank Hanes had went sumwhere when i went up to his house. then i went up to the Chadwicks but they and Parson Otis and Fatty Gilman had went sumwhere but nobody gnew where. then i went home and found that Potter Goram and Chick Chickering had come down with there butterfli nets to get me to go and get sum lait buterflise. i tell you i hipered down to Moultons field and they wasent there and then up to the grove and they wasent there. then i went home feeling pretty loansum.

well there wasent ennything to do for fun so i split sum wood and then mother asted me if i wood screw sum things up in the kitchen to hang close on. so i got the screw driver and went to wirk. while i was wirking Pewt came over. i was awful glad to see Pewt but i thougt he had acked kind of meen to me in not coming over to see me befoar and so i thougt i would punish him a litle befoar i maid up. so i said hi Pewt and went on with my wirk. Pewt sed what are you doing Plupy and i sed saying my prairs before going to bed. then Pewt sed huh and kept quiet and i went on wirking and wisling as if i was aloan. bimbye Pewt sed if you take a hammer and drive the screw in a little way it will taik hold and i sed sort of scornful is that so and he sed yes that is so and if you want to get that screw in this weak you had better do as i say. i dident say ennything only grunted and kep wirking until it broak the head of the screw off then Pewt begun to laff and said there what did i tell you. let me show you how to do it Plupy. i sed supose you think you can bild a barn. Pewt sed peraps i can and i sed sumone is getting pretty smart round here and Pewt said i know a feller whitch aint very smart and i sed well if you dont like what you see round here you know where you can go and Pewt he sed i bet i know where i can go and i am going there two old Plupe and the next tim i come round here again you will know it and i sed no sirre i shant know it for when you come over here again i shall be sumwhere elce.

then Pewt went off hollering

> Plupys mad and i am glad
> and i know what will pleeze him
> taik a nail and scrach his tale
> and hang him up and greece him.

jest as loud as he cood holer and then he hollered you are a old seesand munky and a bristol brick wild man of Bornio, and i hollered silver is better than pewter and who hooked Perry Moultons apples and Pewt hollered back who et them and i shet up becaus i was afrade mother mite hear him.

well after Pewt had went i felt wirse than ever becaus i realy was glad to see him and wanted him to stay and have sum fun but sumhow i coodent help being meen to him. it is funny how a feller will do jest what he dont want to do and the more he dont want to the more he will do it.

well after Pewt went off mad and i took a hammer and done jest what he told me and them screws did jest as he sed they wood and i dident have enny truble. i gues i was a darn fool for sassing Pewt when he was doing me a good tirn but he needent have called me them names at leest he needent have called me them mad. you can call a feller naimes good natured and he jest laffs but if you call a feller the saim naims mad then they is a row and the fellers dont speek enny more.

well tonite Pewt and Beany had all the fellers over to Beanys house having a grate time and mister Watson Beanys father come out and plaid with them jest lika a boy and they had a lot of fun and then mister Watson Beanys father went in and dressed up in an old stovepipe hat and pertended he was a drunk man and he wood stager agenst the fense and they wood plug him with roten tomatose and cucumbers and nock his old stovepipe hat off and squash on his close and he wood chase them and tumble down and you never see sutch fun in your life. i tell you i was jest about crasy to go over there but i coodent becaus me and Beany was mad and Pewt two so i had to stay on my steps and watch them. you never see sutch fun in your life. mister Watson Beanys father is the funniest man i ever see he dont never drink or get drunk but he can ack like a drunk man jest so you wood think he was drunk and maik you kill yourself laffing.

well after it grew dark i went in to study but i felt so loansum that i went up stairs and went to bed. mother came up and asted me if i was sick and i sed no only i dident feal verry well and she wanted to give me sum castor oil but i sed i was all rite. so she went down after she had felt of my head and it was cold so she sed i was all rite only a little tired.

Cele sed she wood do my xamples for me and i cood copy them in the morning. it is awful hard to give up your frends becaus they have a bad effect on you. i bet it is harder than to give up licker after a man has been a drunkerd all his life. it dont seam to be hard for Pewt and Beany to give me up. they seam to have more fun than ever befoar. enny way i have got to get used to it. father says you can get used to enything if you taik time enuf.

October 9, 186—-rany today and windy. about a milion leeves blowed down today. tonite we had a fire in the air tite stove and it seamed moar cheerful. Beany and Pewt coodent have the fellers in Beanys yard. i am still wundering how Beany lerned how to do them xamples. it aint like him to know now. i still feal pretty blew.

October 10, 186— brite and fair. there was a frost last nite. I dident miss today. neether Pewt or Beany spoke to me. tonite i done my choars and went and set on the steps and wached the fellers playing in Beanys yard. i felt pretty bad. father sed what is the matter with you. i sed nothing and he sed you have been acking like a sick cat for a weak why dont you go over and play with the boys and i sed i dont want to. he sed you havent had a fite with Elbridge, Elbridge is Beany you know, and i sed no. then he asted me if i had a fite with Clarence, Clarence is Pewt you know, and i sed no, i havent had enny fie with Pewt, then he went in and set by the table and red the Exeter Newsletter whitch always comes out on Fridays. i went in and went up stairs because we dont have xamples on Saturday only speeking and geogrify.

after i went up stairs i went into the front room. it was warm and the windows was open. father had went out on the front steps and i was setting in the window lissening to the fellers and wishing i was out there with them. bimeby i heard father say to mother Joey what is the matter with Harry laitly. he has been acking nummer than a deef mewt and mother sed i dont know what it is. he has done his choars better than i ever gnew him to do them xcept jest befoar crismas and 4th of July and he eets well but he dont play enny moar and he dont seam like himself enny moar. then father he sed i dont like it. i hoap he isnt going to be a lollypop or a goody good boy. if there is ennything i hait in this wirld it is a miss Nancy sort of boy.

Aunt Sarah she up and sed i gess you needent wurry about any boy of yours being a miss Nancy, George Shute, and father laffed and sed well it dont seam as if i ever cood have a boy like that but you cant be sure. as far as i know there aint enny ministers in my family sence the pilgrim fathers landed on the wild New Ingland shoar. then Aunt Sarah she sed peraps it would have been better if they had been a few and father he sed that may be so but i dout it. then father he sed it aint natural for a boy to set round like a sick hen. either he is thinking up sum deviltry or he is getting to be a lollipop and of the 2 things i ruther it wood be the ferst.

then mother sed i dont quite agree with you George. i dont like a miss Nancy enny moar than you do but i dont beleeve it is nessary for a boy to be thinking up deviltry to be a real boy. then father he sed i gess you was never a boy Joey or you woodent say that. A boy is going to raise tune or he aint a boy and you mite as well put him into skerts to onct. i never gnew a puppy to grow up into a good dog unless he chewed up slippers and spoilt moar things than he was wirth. then mother sed that depends on what you call a good dog. if you meen a dog whitch is all the time fiting that is one thing but if you meen a real good dog that is another thing. then father he sed i woodent give a cent for a dog that cant fite. a god dog that is groan up dont care to fite but will if he has to. and a good man dont cair to but will if he has to. they is a difference between a good boy and a goody good boy. i wood ruther my boy wood git into scraips than not. if he dont i know sumthing is rong with him.

then mother she sed if you like to have him get into scraips why do you get so mad with him and lick him, only mother she sed punnish him, when he gets into scraips and father sed dont you see i cant aprove of his scraips for if i did he wood be in scraips all the time and he wood be if he gnew what i was saying. then father began to laff and to tell what he and Gim Melcher and Bill Yung and Beanys father and Pewts father done when they was boys and he asted if all of them fellers wasent pretty good men and Aunt Sarah sed none of them is mutch to brag of and father laffed and sed that shows you aint a good judge of caracter.

i tell you when i herd what father sed i maid up my mind that i wood maik up with Beany and Pewt and we wood show father and Pewts father and Beanys father that we was jest as lifely as they was when they was boys. then i tell you i felt beter than i had felt for a long while and i am going to bed. to-morrow i will maik up with Pewt and Beany.

October 11, 186—-brite and fair. today i maid up with Pewt and Beany. it wasent near so hard as i thought it wood be. i gess boath of them missed me two but not as mutch as i missed them becaus they had the other fellers. this afternoon we got up a club whitch we call the Terrible 3. i am the president becaus i got it up. Pewt is the secritery becaus he can wright so good and Beany is the tresurer becaus it dont cost ennything to get in and he aint got enny money to taik cair of. the objeck of the club is to do tuf things and not get found out. i aint got time to wright enny moar about it tonite becaus we aint had a reglar meating of the club yet. we are going to have one tomorrow after chirch and wright out a consecration and bi laws. after we have did this things is going to be ifely round here.

October 12, 186—-brite and fair. it is jest raning leeves today. i went to chirch and to sunday school. Beany sed he was going to raise time in chirch so as to lose his gob. he sed a feller whitch was going to be tresurer of the Terible 3 hadent augt to have a chirch gob, but me and Pewt told him he must kep his gob becaus if he wasent going to get caugt when we done tuf things we must be respecktable befoar folks. we told Beany that if he rased time two mutch and a feller hapened to get his windows broak he wood say we fellers done it and then peraps we cood lie out of it and peraps we coodent. so Beany he desided to behaive and to keep his gob, and he done well and only let the wind out of the organ 1 time and that was when he was looking at a rooster fite in old man Elliots yard throug the window, and of coarse when there is a rooster fite or a dog fite or enny kind of a fite a feller has jest got to look at it. the only thing that maid it funier than time was becaus they had got a woman from out of town to sing in the quire and she was singing

the voice of one criing in the wilderniss

and jest then the organ went eooowaugh and sounded like when you step on 40 cats tales to onct and stoped and then begun again and we cood hear Beany pumping as fast as he cood and the old bellose maid a noise just like the braiks on a fire ingine, like this, chunka, chunka, chunka, and everybody laffed and the woman set down mad and woodent sing eny moar.

Chipper and old Hen Dow jawed Beany like time after chirch. Beany he told them why he done it but they dident seam to think that was enny xcuse and kep on jawing him. Chipper he sed he has stood moar from Beany than he had from enny feller and that a house of worship wasent a place for munky shines and this was the last chanct Beany shood have. so Beany kep his gob but he has a narow escaip and will have to be moar cairful nex time.

well after sunday school we met in Beanys barn and rote out the consecration and bi laws. it is a old peeler. i had borrowed sum bi laws of a club father usted to be in and i had rote down a lot of things to put in and Pewt coppied them after we had talked them over becaus Pewt can wright so good. This is what he rote.

Consecration and bi laws of the
Terrible 3.

we Pewt and Beany and Plupy do hearbi asosiate ourselfs together under the corperat naim of the Terible 3.

artickle 1. the object of this asosiasion is to brake windows, to plug green apples and ripe tomatose and roten cucumbers at peeple we dont like or whitch wares there best close on a weak day, or whitch feels two big for his britches. to get even with fellers and with peeple whitch has done rong to us in the past or in the future. wether we have to do it with slingshots or roten egs.

resolvd that the use of slingshots and roten egs is only to be used when enny unusuel or crool rong has been did us. and when the punishment must be sevear.

artickle 2. the main objeck of the members is not to get cougt and evry feller whitch is a member must agree never to betray enny other feller if he gets cougt himself and is licked to maik him tell. and enny feller whitch does tell on another member will be maid to eet a live toad and 4 angel wirms. it is no xcuse if he does it under terible tortures sutch as shaking hands with a pensil between your fingers or putting musterd on your tung or licking you with a bed slot in whitch tacts has been put.

artickle 3. the offisers of the asosiation shall be a president a secritary and a tresurer. the duty of the president shall be to call the meatings of the asosiation. the duty of the secritary shall be to wright down what is did at the meatings. the duty of the treasurer is to take cair of the money of the association.

artickle 4. it dont cost ennything to get into the asosiation. the Terrible 3 is good frends and will stand by eech other as long as live remanes and no money makes anny diference. nobody elce can get in but the Terible 3 at enny prise what ever.

artickle 5. steeling is absolootly forbiddon. this aplise to money, gewils, hens, roosters and chickings, dogs, horses and cattle and ennything whitch peeple has in there houses and barns, but does not apli to apples, pares straberries and frutes in their seeson befoar they has been pictd and put in the house or barn and nothing in this consecration shall be considered as hendering enny one of the Terible 3 from pluging ennything at cats dogs or other animals.

artickle 6. at the end of the asosiasion whitch will come when enny of the members is ded or in jale the propity of the asosiasion shall be divided equil between sutch of the members as aint ded or in jale and the records of the asosiation if there is enny shall be birnt and distroid.

bi laws

I. evry member shall be reddy to fite for another member at a moments notise.

II. evry member shall be reddy to lie for another member when ever he can help him by liing. if he can help him by teling the trooth he will be xpected to do so if he can.

III. if a feller gets cougt he is xpected to lay it on to sum feller whitch is likely to do them things whitch he is cougt for doing.

IV. the fellers whitch is most likely to do the things whitch a feller is most likely to get cougt for doing is Fatty Gilman, Skinny Bruce,

Tady Fenton, Jack Melvin, Whack, Pozzy and Bug Chadwick, Fatty Melcher, Pop Clark, Hiram Mingo, Ben Rundlett, Ed Tole and several others.

V. evry member has go to commit them naims to memory and keep them at his tungs end becaus he mite need them at enny time.

VI. as far as posiable members must keep out of enny trubble with wimmen. the Terible 3 does not wage war against wimmen. of coarse when a woman has got a husband whitch the Terible 3 has ennything agenst she must taik her chanct but she wont be hirt if she keeps her fingers out of the pye. i have never knew a woman to do that in our lifes. it aint our falt that she is his wife. she done it herself.

VII. as far as posiable the Terible 3 will try to keep out of trubble in school. it aint that we are scart of old Francis but it seams sumtimes as if he had got eys in the back of his hed and gnew evrything a feller thinks befoar he thinks it.

then we all sined. we was going to have 3 or 4 more bi laws but we dident know enny moar roman numbers and you have got to have figger numbers for the artickles and roman numbers for the bi laws. after we had sined it i thougt we cood have got them from the clock. we dident think of that.

after we had sined it Pewt gave it to me to keep as i am the president. he sed he had augt to keep them becaus he is secritary but i told him that artickle 3 of the consecration sed the duty of the secretary was to wright what was did at the meatings and dident say he was to keep the paper. so Pewt give in.

Oct. 13, 186—-brite and fair. the secritary of the Terible 3 got licked in school today becaus he sed geogrify is the sience of numbers and the art of compewting by them. he told old Francis he wasent thinking and old Francis he give him a licking to maik him think. tonite the Terible 3 comited our ferst crime. this is the way we done it. we agread to be studding our lessons at 8 oh clock. when it struck 8 we wood go out for a drink or sumthing and meat on Elm strete jest behine Pewts and Beanys house. Pewt and Beany had got a pile of ripe tomatose. then we would ding old William Hobbs door bell and when he come to the door we wood paist him. He always drives us out of his yard so we done it. when it struck 8 oh clock i sed i forgot to shet up my hens and a skunk may come round. Keene sed i will help you. i sed no i will do it. what would you do if we met a skunk. so i went down and hipered over to Elm Strete. Pewt and Beany was there with their hands full of tomatose. Pewt tiptode up and rung the bell. in a minit old Hobbs come to the door with a candle shaded with his hand. as soon as he come out we let ding as hard as we cood eech one 3 or 4 tomatose. one nocked the candle out of his hand and put it out. one hit him square in the mouth and squashed. 2 or 3 hit him in other places and the rest squashed on the house. i wish you cood herd him spitt and sware and holler. jest as soon as we pluged him we started running towards front strete and then went behine the Unitarial chirch throug a hole in Fifields fense into Beanys yard. i wasent away from the house more than 3 minits. when i came in mother sed did you shet the door to the hen coop and i sed yes. i did shet it becaus i thought she mite ast me.

in about half an hour old man Hobbs rung our door bell and asted mother where i was. she sed do you want to see him and he sed where has he been tonite and she sed he has been in studdying all the evening ever sence supper and he sed are you sure and she sed why yes i have been here myself. then he sed well sum boys came to my house and rung my door bell and when i come to the door they threw roten vegitables at me and asaulted me and if i can find out ther edentitty i am going to persecute them to the xtent of the law and send them to jale.

mother she sed it is a shaim and i certainly hoap you will find out who they are and i am very glad to say that my son had nothing to do iwth it and i am sure he wood not do ennything of the kind. so old Hobbs he went away and mother came in and told us. she sed he hadent quite got all of the tomatose out of his wiskers but she hoped he wood ketch them. i hoap so two over the left. it may lern old Hobbs a lesson if he isent two old to learn. i am afrade he is.

October 14, 186—-i have got 2 horks. Potter Goram give them to me. they is full groan and verry hansum. one is a hen hork and the other a red taled hork. gess what i naimed them. one is Hork and the other Spitt. mother sed those were dredful naims but i think they are prety good ones. i feed them on meat and fishes and rats and mice. if you poak them with a stick they grab it with his claus and hiss like a snaik. there eys is yellow. i dont let folks poak them.

tonite i called a meating of he Terible 3. i had rote the record of what we had did and Pewt had coppied it. i thougt i had better wright it becaus i can spel so mutch beter than Pewt.

well Pewt read the record and Beany reported that there wasent enny money in the tresury. then i asted if ennybody had ennything to say and Beany sed that we had better paist old decon Aspinwall next for he was so meen. i was afrade he wood lay it onto me becaus i had trubble with him 2 times. then Pewt sed we cood nale up a sine in front of his house sassing him, but i had done that onct for a circus. so we desided to lay for him sum time but not yet. ennyway we have got him marked.

so after supper we took a few grean apples and our sticks and went into Pewts back yard behind the trees and plugged sum apples as hard as we cood without ameing. we fired them in the direxion of J. Albert Clarks house becaus he had ordered me and Beany out of his yard one day jest for nothing.

we wood all plug together jest as hard as we cood plug and then lissen hard. we cood tell by the sound when they wood hit on the roofs or not. bimeby we herd the gingle of glass 2 times. then we begun to play coram and kep hollering and laffin. then we herd J. Ward Levitt holler who in hell is firing rocks through my winders. then he hollered to father and sed George look here and see what your dam boy has been up to and we herd father say what is it Ward and Ward sed he has broak 2 winders in my shop and you have got to pay for them. then father sed all rite. if he done it i will pay but if he hasent done it i wont. so ferst father hollered for me and i dident hear him. then they went over to Beanys and i wasent there and Beanys mother sed i hadent been there. then they come through old Mrs. Seeveys yard and then into Pewts and we were playing coram. then J Ward sed here are the devils and father sed dident you hear me holler and i sed did you holler and looked at him sirprized and father sed i hollered louder than a steem wissel and i sed we were playing coram and making so mutch noise that i gess it drownded your holler out. then he sed how long have you been here and i sed ever sence suppr.

then father sed Ward says you broak 2 winders in his shop, and i sed how cood i when i have been here evry minit. and father sed are you sure you havent been out of this yard sence you come here, now dont you lie to me and i sed hoap to die and cross my throte have i

Pewt have i Beany and Pewt and Beany both hoaped to die and crossed there throtes.

then father sed there Ward you see they coodent have did it for it is twict as far as enn one of them can throw and Ward he sed i dont know about that. then father sed try boys and see how far you can throw and try as hard as you can. so i pict up a rock and let ding and nearly throwed my arm out of goint and it went clear across Mrs. Seeveys yard into Beanys and then Pewt he throwed clear over Beanys house into old Heads yard and beat me and Beany throwed into his yard but not so far as i did. then old Ward he sed we dident try and father sed if you can throw across Mrs. Seeveys yard and into Watsons yard, Watson is Beanys father you know, i will pay for them winders even if Harry dident brake them.

then old J Ward he sed all rite George i will show these boys what i can do and he took off his long taled coat and roled up his sleaves and hunted round for a rock and then he let ding and the rock went sideways rite towards Mrs. Seeveys house and went rite throug one of her kichen winders and the minit it went in she come out yapping who has broak my winder and old J. Ward stood with his mouth open and one hind leg in the air where he had drawed it up when he saw the rock going towerds the winder. so when she hollered who broak my winder he put his hind leg down and stutered and sed i gess i done it maam and she sed what did you do it for? aint you got enny better business than to go round throwing rocks throug peeples winders and he sed i was jest showing these boys how to throw a stone and she sed well if they cant throw enny better than you can i gess you havent showed them mutch. now if you will show me about 25 cents for that winder and i will say no moar about it. so old J. Ward pade her 25 cents and she went in. then father sed are you sure you dident brake them winders yourself Ward you seam to be a good shot. old J. Ward laffed and sed well George i gess these boys dident do it, but i am going to find out who done it if it takes me a weak. i bet that out of a John Bowley done it. John Bowley is Squawboo Bowley you know, or posiably that Peenut Perkins or Johnny Kelly. so old J. Ward is going to pich into them.

enny way we dident meen to brake his winders and the Terible 3 hasent got ennything agenst old J. Ward for he is a good feller and dont never drive us out of his Carrige shop, but if we had sed we done it it mite let the hoal thing out. so i gess we done rite but we will even up with old J. Albert sum time. his time will come unless he changes his ways.

October 15, 186—-brite and fair. wenesday and so no school this afternoon. as it is warm the fish bit prety well and i went down to my boat and cougt ten shiners and a lot of minnis. it is prety lait for them. then i fed Hork and Spitt and you had augt to have see them eat. i dont know what i shall do when the fish stop biting. rats is scarce and i cant aford chickings.

this afternoon after i had come back from fishing we had a meating of the Terible 3. we met at Pewts shop. Pewt read the report whitch i had rote for him and he had coppied. then we talked about wether we had augt to use sling shots xcept in xstream cases. we desided never to use sling shots in a croud and never to ame hier than a fellers hind leg xcept when he is tirned back to for fear of puting out his ey. and we desided never to fire a sling shot without ameing nor rocks neether. but grean apples and all other vegtibles including both stail and roten egs espeshionally goos egs whitch is hard to get and ded fish whitch you swing round your tale by the head, no i meant whitch you swing round your head by the tale and let ding is all rite to plug without amein becaus they wont do enny harm and cant put out a fellers ey.

i am going to have that rote into the record.

October 16, 186—-brite and fair. Spitt cougt a almost full groan chicking today. the chicking stuck his head between the slats and Spitt grabed him with his claus and pulled him the rest of the way in and toar him in peaces and et most of him. it is verry xpensive to keep two mutch stock but i hait to let eether of them go. Hork is all rite and Spitt is all rite but Hork and Spitt together is moar than 1 feller can feed unless he is a butcher or a fishcart man or a rat ketcher.

tonite the Terible 3 dident comit enny crime becaus Billy Morris Nigger ministrils give a show in the town hall and we all went. at 1 oh clock there was a parade and there band plaid. it is a ripper and can play almost as loud as the Exeter Band. tonite we all went. it was the funiest show i ever went to. it beat Comical Brown all to peaces and the orchistry was splendid. They sung shoo fli dont bodder me and little Maggy May, Way down upon the Swany river and Massa is in the cold cold ground and they dansed clog danses and had funny direlogs. i tell you it was fine. so the Terible 3 dident do nothing. somehow when a feller is laffin he doesent feel like comitting crimes unless it is funny ones.

October 17, 186—-missed in grammer today and got licked. not very bad only he shook me round until he toar my coller and neckti off. i jest wish the Terible 3 wood plug old Francis sum time with bricks.

old J. Ward Levitt has found out who broak his winders and has got his pay for them. he come over tonite and told me and father about it. he sed he went down to Squawboo Bowleys and asted him about it and Squawboo proofed that he was down to Charles Grants store on Hemloc square with Peenut Perkins all that evening. then he went down to old Heads house and asted two stewcats about it and they sed they never done it then J. Ward he told them they wood pay him for them winders or he wood go to doctor Soule of the academy about it and them fellers sed they never done it but had ruther pay for 2 winders than to have doctor Soule asting them questions, and so J. Ward sed they pade him 50 cents for the 2 winders and 50 cents for the trubble he had in detecking them and maiking them confess. he sed they sed that they dident confess and never done it but he sed if they was onnest fellers they woodent pay for brakeing winders whitch they hadent never broak and he sed aint that rite Geroge? to father and father he laffed and sed well i aint so sure about that. i was in the academy under docter Soule and gess there wasent enny time i was ther after the ferst weak that i woodent rather pay for 2 windows than to have docter Soule ast me questions about what i had did. but i gess these fellers must have did it or they woodent have pade for it.

Aunt Sarah sed father was xpelled from the academy twict. i asted him what he was xpelled for. he sed the ferst time was a case of religious persecution. i asted why they was persecuting him and he sed he and another feller thougt the students was having to pay too mutch atension to morning prairs in the chapil and so he and the other feller screwed up the doors of the chapil one nite and the nex morning they coodent get into the chapil for 2 days and they found out that he and the other feller had bougt sum screws. so they persecuted him for that and xpelled him.

then i asted him why he got xpelled the 2nd time and he sed it was edjucasional persecution of the wirst kind. i asted him what they done to persecute him that way and he sed that docter Soule marked all the fellers down awful low and it dident make enny difference how hard he studded none of the fellers cood get a good mark. father sed it was dredful the amount of whale oil he birnt in lamps nites studding his greke and latin. he thinks he must have birnt about 2 hoal whales full but it dident do enny good. he never cood get a good mark. well docter Soule kep his marking sheets in his desk and eech day he marked the felers down feerful low and locked his sheets in the desk and at the end of the day he wood give the shets to anothr teecher to add them up and give out a list of the best scolars.

well father and another feller got a kee that wood fit the lock of that desk and evry day they wood get the sheet and mark evry feller 100 percent and docter Soule never looked at it and give them to the other teecher to add up and evrybody got perfict marks and evrybody sed it was the best class in the school.

well bimeby one day father and the other feller marked themselfs 125 percent and when the other teecher added the marks up he found sumthing was rong. so he spent a weak adding and substrackting and multipliing and dividing and reduceing to the leest common denominator and invirtin the diviser and perceeding as in multiplication and finding the leest common multipel of and xtracking the squair root of and at last he maid up his mind that there was a niger in the woodpile.

so he took his figgers to old docter Soule and they set a trap and cougt father and the other feller and they xpelled them and that was the last of father in the academy. but while he was there he was verry poplar becaus they wasent ennything he woodent do for his classmaits.

so i gess he was rite when he told old J. Ward what he did about old docter Soule. father sed he tride to get back onct moar and he thougt they had augt to have gave him one moar chanct. if he cood have been xpelled onct moar he cood beet enny feller whitch ever went to the academy he was verry mutch disapointed when they woodent give him another try so he cood be xpelled onct moar.

so when we had the nex meating of th Teribl 3 i wanted them to mark old docter Soule to paist sum nite but they woodent do it becaus they sed we was all townies and we woodent notise the academy. Pewt and Beany was gelous becaus Pewts father and

Beanys father hadent never been xpelled from nowhere. they thougt i was showing off but i wasent.

October 17, 186—-brite and fair and hot as summer. it has been hot for almost a weak. Rob Bruce, Skinnys brother and Dan Casidy went in swiming yesterday. they sed it was bully but i bet it was cold. tonite after school Pewt maid sum sines whitch we put up after dark. one we put up in front of old Ike Shutes door. it sed bewair Ike the Terible 3 is on your trale. that will be enuf to keep Ike in nites. Ike drives us out of his yard when he sees us.

another one we put on Bill Eldriges door. it sed the vengence of the Terible 3 will folow You Bill until you are ded or in jale. the last one we put on Peeliky Tiltons granfathers door becaus he put tin cans and broaken glass bottels and old hoopskerts and wire into the swiming hole at sandy bottom and we cant swim there enny moar. i dont know jest what we will do to him. it seams as if slingshots or roten egs aint bad enuf. we will try to scair him to deth ferst and then we will do sumthings to him that he will never forget in his life even if he lives to be 200 years old. the sine sed this old man Tilton say your prairs for the Terible 3 has got you on their list. when litening strikes it leaves no traices of its victims. bewair bewair.

Pewt rote them with sum stencil plaits his father has got so nobody will know his hand wrighting.

October 18, 186—-this morning we had speaking in school. i spoke Horatias at the brige. it made me think of the Terible 3 when it sed

> the three stood carm and staitly
> and looked upon there foes
> and a grat shout of laffter
> from all the vangard rose

but all the saim they nocked the stuffing out of Aunus from grean Tifernum and Seius and the other fellers and it wasent enny laffin matter for them and it wont be enny laffin matter with the Terible 3. old man Tilton dident laff this morning when he see that sine on his door. he has laid it onto old Marco Bazzris Wadley and Jack Flinn and Gimmy Fitsgerald and Moog Carter all ready, and Luke Manix two and old Ike Shute has had old Kize and old Swane the Poliseman up to see about his sine and old Bill Eldrige has been to see 2 lawyers Alvy Wood and Jug Stickney. everybody but them is laffin and wundering who the Terible 3 is. sum of them may find out sum day.

well this afternoon me and Pewt and Beany went up river fishing. we dident xpect to get ennything it was so lait in the fall but Hork and Spitt hadent been fed for 2 days. we got a lot of shiners and perch and jest befoar we come back we got the bigest snaping tirtle i ever see in my life. it was a ripper and the madest one i ever see. it snaped rite and left and wood throw his head rite back on his shell trying to grab us. we had hard wirk to get a peace of closeline round his hind leg. the only way we cood do it was to let it bite a stick and hold on.

we had desided to use a slingshot on old man Tilton sum day when he was bending over a sawhorse and his britches were tite but Pewt sed it wood be a good thing to scair him to deth with the snaping tirtle ferst. so we are going to tie him to old man Tiltons doornob sum nite and ring the doorbell. we coodent do it tonite becaus evrybody goes down town Saturday nite to the stores and sets up lait having baths and things. but look out for yourself mister old man Tilton for the Terible 3 in on your trale.

we xpect a bizzy weak nex weak.

Oct. 19, 186—-Sunday. rainy and windy. had to go to chirch. the only fun i had was to see peeples umbrellas blow rongside out and to hear them sware. sum of them was chirch members two. they did not belong to the Unitarial chirch.

Oct. 20, 186—-rany as time. i never gnew it to rane harder. evryone had on rubber boots and umbrelas. the wind blew terible and all the leeves is gone and sum branches of trees is blew down. Buldy Tasker pushed me into the gutter in front of old Gim Ellersons lacksmith shop and i went in over my rubber boots. when i got to school i puled off my boots and poared out the water and there was about 4 quats in eech boot. it taiks a long time to dry rubber boots. they say the best way is to fill them full of otes and after the otes has been in about a day or 2 poar out the otes and the boots is dry and the otes is wet. so when i got home i was going to do it but there wasent moar than a pec of otes in the baril and Nellie had to be fed so i had to put the boots upside down behine the stove in the kitchen. the Terible 3 had a meating and went down to see our snaping tirtle. he was there all rite hiched by his old hine leg to a tree and he was out of site in a pudle of water that the rane had made. we pulled him out by the hine leg and he was awful mad and claued and scrached and snaped. so we let him go back in his pudle after we had saw that the closeline was all rite. i bet we will maik old man Tilton gump out of his britches when he sees that old tirtle hanging to his doorgnob. i hope he will for enny man whitch will fill up a swimming hole with old tin cans and glass had augt to be bit by a ratlesnaik.

October 21, 186—-it has stoped raning today. for a wunder neether me or Beany or Pewt missed in our lesons. it dont verry often hapen that way. i think old Francis thougt we was playing sum sort of a trick on him for he acked sort of quear and looked at us sort of hard. tonite we aranged to meat at Pewts at 8 oh clock. after school we got a meel bag and went down for our snaping tirtle. it took nearly a hour to get him into the bag. ferst we had to ty up his mouth becaus we only want to scair old man Tilton and not to kill him. it took a haff hour to do that. we never cood have did it if it hadent ben for Pewt who can ty gnots like a sailer. ferst we got the old tirtle mad and then we give him a stick to bite and then i pulled at it and Beany pulled at the roap on his hine leg. of coarse the snaper woodent let go of the stick and when his head was out strait Pewt put a noos round his mouth and wound it round and round like ganging a fishhook on a line and he tide that old tirtles mouth up titer than a drumhead.

then we tride to get him in the bag but it was all we cood do he claud so. bimby we got him in. then we tide the bag under a bush down behine old Perry Moultons yard. then we went home. i split up my kinlins and done my choars and studded till 8 oh clock and then mother sed i cood go down town with Beany. so i went over to Beanys and it was dark. so we got Pewt and went down and got the bag and carried it up Court strete and throug old Nat Gordons woods until we got to the feeld oposite old man Tiltons house.

it was a awful lug and i bet we put it down to rest 50 times but bimeby we got it there. then we tride to shaik the old snaper out of the bag and it seamed as if we never cood get him out. bimeby we got him out and lit sum maches to see his mouth was tide up tite and it was and the stick was still there he coodent spitt it out. gosh but he was mad and tride to snap. there was a lite in old man Tiltons house and we cood see him setting by a table with a red cloth and a lamp with a red wick reading. sumwhere in the back of the house was another lite and we could hear Peeliky Tiltons uncles practising band tunes on their horns. they was making a feerful noise so nobody heard us when we 3 tide the snapper to the dorgnob. it was all we cood do he claued so. then when we had him hanging head downwerds we rung the bell as hard as we cood and hipered acrost the strete and hid in the bushes behine the fense.

we cood see old man Tilton put down his paper and holler sumthing. i gess he told Peeliky Tiltons uncles to stop their noise. ennyway it stoped and he lit a little tin lamp and come to the door and opened it. we cood hear the old tirtle scraching at the door and banging his head agenst it as he tried to snap and the old man heard it and when he opened the door he looked round throug his old specks and dident see ennything and then he steped out on the porch and stuck his hed round the door and i gess it was lucky he dident take the big lamp for when he see that old snaper swinging this way and that way clauing and snaping he let out a yell you cood heard for 3 miles and droped the lamp and almost tirned a back sumerset he tride so hard to get back into the house and slamed the door. then we heard him hollering for Peeliky Tiltons uncles and we cood see them come piling into the room and evryone talked. then they come out of the side door. Peeliky Tiltons uncle had a lantirn and a ax and his uncle George had a shot gun and a tin lamp and his uncle Warren had a pichfork and a torchlite percession torch and old man Tilton was looking out of the window. Ed went first with the lantern and when he saw what it was he sed it is a snaping tirtle as big as a wash boiler. sum darn fool has tide it to the gnob. so George sed sumone cut the roap and we will get him and Warrin he sed look out them snapers will taik a mans hine leg off at 1 snap and Ed sed hell i aint afrade and he cut the roap with his ax and the old snaper fell on the steps and begun to craul off and Ed grabed the roap and yanked him onto the sidewaulk and he sed hold the lite Warrin and let the snaper bite a stick and i will cut his hed off. so Warrin he held a lite and George got a stick and poaked him and the old snaper snaped but dident ketch hold and Ed he sed that is a hell of a snaper. so George poaked him again and he kep snaping and bimeby Ed sed sum feller has tide up his mouth with a stick in it. so then nobody was afrade and they all gethered round and Peeliky and his father come out of their house and old man Tilton come out and sed things have come to a pretty pass if a man cant go to his door without being et alive by a snaping tirtle or knawed by a rampaiging wilcat or pizened by a hoopskert.

he meant a hoop snaik but he was xcited, and if the polise dident do there duty he wood put it in the hands of the county solissiter and see is respectible citisens cood be et and lose their lifes without nobody doing ennything to stop it. and he sed do we live in Rooshy or Prooshy and dont a man have enny petection of the law? and he waulked up and down the porch and banged his cain and hollered and while he was hollering Ed and George and Warrin and Peeliky and Peelikys father was taiking the old snaper into the back yard and they cut his head off and Ed told Peeliky that the head woodent die for 7 days. then they come back and told the old man to shet up and Ed sed they was going to have tirtle soop and fride chicking, and rost beef and boiled ham and sossige and quale on tost and clamb chowder and pigs feet and pork scraps and hogs head cheze all out of that tirtle. but the old man kep a hollering and asking if he lived in Rooshy and Ed sed the old man will feal better tomorrow when he has drunk about a quat of soop and et 4 or 5 pounds of diferent kinds of meet from that old snaper.

well bimeby they went in and the old man went in and set down and they begun to play on their horns and we clim over the fence and went home. i gess we scart the old man most to deth. if you had saw him let out the yell and heard him tirn the back somerset you wood have thougt so. we aint throug with him yet. a man whitch will stop up a swiming hol with tin cans and broaken glass aint going to get off with lesson. and wire two whitch is cumtimes wirse. and hoopskerts.

then we all went down town and come up throug Coart Strete laffing and talking about what we see in the store winders so our folks wood know we had been down town. mother sed i was prety lait and sed that father sed i hadent augt to be out so lait but she told him i asted if i cood go and she sed yes. she told me i must come home erlier next time. father had went to bed so i dident see him and he dident yip.

it was the most sucesful meating the Terible 3 has had. i have got to wright out the report for Pewt becaus i can spel so mutch beter than Pewt can. so i cant wright moar tonite in this diry.

October 28, 186—-today the ferst thing i see was old man Tilton coming down town with his old cain. he glore at me when i met him and i sed how do you do mister Tilton and he sed how do how do and waulked on. so i know he doesnt suspeck us. i bet he woodent say how do to Gimmy Fitzgerald or Moog Carter or Luke Mannix or Ticky Moses. i wached him and he went into the polise stasion. then he come out and talked with old Swane and old Mizzery Durgin the polise oficers. his naim is Ezry but we call him Mizzery. he is the feller that throwed me out of the town hall the nite father was going to maik a speach and dident dass to. old man Tilton pounded his cain on the ground and hollered. i coodent hear what he sed except Rooshy and Prooshy so i gess he was triing to find out where he lived becaus he wanted to know last nite and nobody told him. i gess he hasent et enny of that soop yet. i wish we cood have kep that tirtle. it wood have fed Hork and Spitt for 2 weaks. i cougt a rat today. an old linger and they toar him up and et him. Spitt had the ferst whack at him and i thougt he wasent going to leeve no coar so i poaked a part of it out with a stick and gave it to Hork. if i kep Hork and Spitt together they wood eet eech other up. i wunder if they wood be ennything left when they got throug.

ennyway a bullfrog can eet another bullfrog as big as he is. the one that gets the first snap gets the other and swalows him down his gozzle with his feet sticking out of the corner of his mouth. A bullfrog swalows the other bullfrog hoal. he chews him up inside like a hen or a boar constricter only he dont squash him ferst. i am glad i am not a bullfrog and havent enny teeth in my stomack. how cood a dentist pull a tooth in a fellers stomack if it aiked. how cood a feller tell wether it was a tooth aik or a stomack aik. wood a feller die if he maid a mistaik and had a dentist pull a tooth whitch was in his stomack when it dident aik but his stomack did. if i was a bullfrog i shood like to know them things. but i aint a bullfrog and i shant have enny teeth in my stomack unless when i am old and have false teeth i swalow them when i am aslep as old man Collins did onct.

tonite we had company. Aunt Mary and Charles and Helen and Cad Smith and Steve and Ann Maria Piper and Annie Piper, and so i coodent go out after supper but had to stay in and hear Keene and Cele sing. i can hear them enny day and i had agreed to go out with Pewt and Beany and try to brake sum of J. Albert Clarks windows to pay for telling father when i let out his rooster to fite mine and mine licked his. if his had licked mine old J. Albert woodent have yipped. i dont blaim him for being mad becaus i let them fite when he wasent there to see and becaus mine licked but no feller that is a real feller will go tattle taleing to a fellers father and get him kep in the yard a hoal day. if he had given me a bat in the ear or had hit me a paist with his cain i woodent have caired but a feller that tells on another has got sumthing to learn and that is what the Terible 3 is for. to lern fellers to behave.

so i coodent go out and Pewt and Beany sed they wood try to do it without me. they sed they wood go up to Pewts yard again and wood try sum grean apples on a stick and aim more to the rite than they did when they broak old J. Ward Levitts windows whitch the stewdcats paid for brakeing. so i kep my ey pealed becaus J. Albert lives in the other side of our house and i gnew if ennyone broak his winders old J. Albert wood come piling in to tell father it was me and father cood tell him he was a dam lier becaus i wood be there with father all the time and father wood know i hadent went out for a minit.

so i set in the parlor and father told the story about the feller whitch got the long hair in his mouth and lots of stories that maid us nearly kill ourselfs laffing. then Cele and Keene sung flow gently sweet Afton and pass under the road and we shall meat but we shall miss him and my mother bids me bang my hair and then father maid me sing alone. i hait to sing alone. i cood have sung with Keene but he maid me sing alone. i sed what shall i sing and he sed sing ennything. so i sung a new virse of if ever i ceese to love. it goes this way

if ever i ceese to love
if ever i ceese to love
may Horris Greelys cat
have kittens in his hat
if ever i ceese to love

well father and Steve and Ann Maria and Aunt Sarah and Aunt Mary and Charles and mother all laffed but Cele and Keene and Annie Piper sed i was very disgusting. ennyway father sed i cood sing ennything.

well after i had sung Cele and Keene were playing a peace about Napolion crossing the Alps when there was a big gingle of glass and a hard apple came wizzing throug the window and came within a inch of taiking Steve on the snoot. Keene gave a screech and evryone gumped up jest as another hit the side of the house bang. father was out of the house and down the steps in 2 minits and i after him. the stewdcats in old mister Heads house were setting by their table studding in there shert sleaves and we heard sum one down the strete and father hipered down strete and i after him. we met Nipper Brown and his father and father he sed have you met enny fellers Gus and Nippers father he sed yes 2 fellers ran down Clifford Strete and me and father went down Clifford strete and coodent see enny fellers. so we went back and i picked up a rock and put it in my pocket. when i ran out after father i picked up the apple and nobody had seen it. i gnew if father see that apple with a hole in it he wood know it was throwed with a stick and he wood know in a minit who broak old J. Ward Levitts winders.

so when we come back to the parlor they sed that 2 more rocks had struck the house while we was gone and i pertended to pick up the rock i had brougt in under the otterman. father sed if that rock had hit you Steven it wood have cooked your goos. and Ann Maria sed it is a mersy it dident and Aunt May sed this is a serius matter George and father sed it is more than that Mary it is a dam outrage and he and Charles went out again and i folowed them. ferst they went over to Beanys and asted his father if he had saw ennyone. he sed he hadent. then father asted where Elbrige was. Elbrige is Beany you know and he sed he was up to Pewts painting sumthing in the shop. so father come back. he was pretty mad and sed he wood give 100 dollers to find out who throwed them rocks. and he wood like to know what the polisemen was for enyway. so he and Charles and Steve talked about how bad the town was run and what a tuf set of rowdies there was now a days and how mutch better it was in the old days. then father he sed a few days ago sum one put a notise up on cousin Isaks house sined by the Terible 3 and Ike hadent been down town sence and hadent been out day times without having old mother Moulton come in and set with his wife while he was gone. he sed Ike had got a pistol and was going to lode it only he dident know whitch end of it loded and his wife was moar scart of the pistol than she was of the Terible 3 whoever the misable cusses was. father sed that old mother Moulton was moar pertection than 5 pistols and 2 bull dogs and he wood pity enny Terrible 3 or Terible 300 whitch wood dass to interfear with her.

then old Steve he sed he had heard of sum things the desperrit villanes had did. they had tide a snaping tirtle to the doorgnob of old mister Tilton and he had been pretty badly bit by him and that docter Perry and docter Swet and docter Perrum had all been called and it was moar than a hour befoar they stoped the flow of blood. i told them i guess that wasent so for i see him down town the next day all rite. i sed the fellers was talking it over at school and Luke mannix sed that the fellers that tide the snaper to the doorgnob had tide up his mouth. he sed he see the snapers head after Ed Tilton Peeliky Tiltons uncle had cut it off and its mouth was tide up with a cord.

Steve sed a feller mite jest as well be bit as scart to deth and Charles Smith sed that may be so cussin Stefen but if i had to be boath i wood ruther be one and i wood ruther be scared to deth becaus you cood get over being scart to deth but you mite not get over being bit if you had a hine leg or arm bit off. ennyway he sed it was time that the orthoritys of the town got together and offered a reward for ennybody whitch wood ketch those fellers.

father sed onct he and Gim Melcher and Bill Young usted to get a pocket full of gravil and when the old fellers was setting round the stove in the stores smoaking and spitting and talking the fellers wood open the stoar door and plug a handful of gravil in and slam the door and run. they done that for quite a while and bimeby old Boss Langly whitch kep a store down by great brige offered a reward of 10 dollers to ennyone whitch wood ketch them. so he hid 2 nites oposite his store and neerly froze to deth for it was in november and a cold nite. bimeby father and Bill and Gim come along and they all got ready. father sed he peeked into the store and see all the old pods setting there and he opened the door and they all pluged the gravil and started to run and run rite into Boss arms and Boss grabed father by one neck and Gim by the other and he waulked them down to fathers fathers house and sent for old Dan Melcher and he came hipering up from his house with his coat tales floating in the breaz. well after they had talked about an hour fathers father and old Dan Melcher paid 10 dollers to old Boss Langly and agreed to tan the hide off of father and Gim if old Boss woodent persecute and woodent tell the other store keepers who pluged the gravil. and fathers father tanned the hide off of father and Gims father tanned the hide off of Gim and Bill got off becaus old Boss dident have but 2 hands to grab with an had put his falce teeth in a glass of water behine the stove and he coodent hold Bill without teeth or he wood have got Bill two, and father and Gim wasent tattletales.

father had sed he thought old Boss got prety good interest for nothing. he got 10 dollers and dident have to pay enny reward and had the fun of ketching them and the way they put it on showed that they liked to do it. so evrybody was satisfide xcept father and Gim. then Aunt Mary she sed well i guess you desirved it George and father laffed and sed i gess i desirved a good deal moar than i ever got Aunt Mary. father had augt to have licked me 10 times as often as he did. and then Hellen Smith sed evrybody tells me George that you was the meanest boy in the town and father sed no Hellen i dont think i was meen. i was bad enuf god knows but i always had lots of frends and kep them and a meen feller never has frends. and Hellen she sed well if you wasent a meen boy i shood like to know what a meen boy was and father he sed a meen boy or man or girl or woman is one whitch does meen things to another or says meen things about them. i dont know whitch is the wirst but i gess the one whitch says meen things about peeple. so Hellen she set up and nobody sed ennything for 2 minits. then Keene got up and went to the piano and set down and sung

i'm the girl that's gay and happy
where so ear i chanct to be
and there's sumthing i will tell you
if you will but list to me

i tell you Keene is rite on hand when there is ennything going on. bimeby they went home and i went upstairs. i wonder what Pewt and Beany will say when they find out that they broak fathers winders insted of old J. Alberts. it seams funny to have to pay Pewts father for putting in new panes of glass in plaice of them whitch Pewt broak. if Pewt can do this evry nite he can keep the old man bizzy all the time and make a pile of money.

October 24, 186—-brite and fair and frost last nite. father waked me up hollering up the stairs. he sed come down here quick so i piled out of bed and put on my close as lifely as i cood and went down 3 steps at a time. when i got there father told me to come out in front of the house and to look and i done it and there on old J. Alberts side of the house was a sine whitch sed

J. Albert Clark we have broak your winders. this is jest a beginning, moar anon. bewair. bewair the Terible 3.

i looked as sirprised as i cood and sed gosh father then it was the Terible 3 and they was trying to get even with J. Albert insted of you. i wunder what he has did to them. but father sed i dont cair what he has did to them it cant go on this way verry long befoar sumone will be in jale. when he sed that i felt as if i dident have enny stomack. then he hollered for J. Albert and old J. Albert come down and when he saw the sine and father had told him about the broaken winder he sed he shood go down town to the polise stasion and make a complaint and see if innosent peeple aint going to have enny pertection under the law.

then father sed have you did ennything rong to ennyone Albert whitch mite want to get even with you and old J. Albert he sed he hadent done rong to a living sole as far as he gnew and he sed i gess George they must have got in the rong side of the house and they ment it for you insted of me and father sed that may be so Albert but it is almity quear that they shood call me J. Albert Clark and hang the sine on your side of the house and J. Albert dident know what to say to this and so he sed i gess that is quear but peeple do quear things sumtimes. then father sed have you heard how they hung a snaping tirtle on old man Tiltons doorgnob and rung his bell and he went to the door and got so badly bit that it took 3 docters to sow him up. and old J. Albert sed no i dident hear of it George. is it trew? and father sed i was told so last nite and i understand other peeple has been warned and assaulted, and in evry case it has been a prety meen man. and J. Albert sed well i dont know what ennyone has got agenst me and if necesery i shall have a poliseman stay here nites and father sed it looks to as if it was only the beginning of sum prety desperit work but if ennything happens jest gnock on the wall and i will come in on the gump.

and old J. Albert sed thank you George i know i can alwys relie on you and father sed you can Albert you can but i am afrade you are in for sumthing verry serius but we must hoap for the best. so then we went in to breckfast and when we got in father began to laff and sed there i have give miss Nancy sumthing to wurry about to pay him for rasing my rent last month. he wont dass to go down town nites enny moar than old Ike Shute.

i sed to father dont you think the Terible 3 will do sumthing feerful to him and father sed no they may roten eg him or sumthing like that but they wont hirt him. i sed do you supose it is big fellers or little fellers and father sed it must be big fellers becaus little fellers coodent ty up a snaping tirtles mouth and coodent ty him to a doorgnob. i figger it is sum big rowdys that want to be smart. it must be sum fellers that aint been to school mutch for that sine is spelt rong in 2 or 3 plaices. so i dident say enny moar and the hack come for father and he got in and went to the trane and i felt better.

After breckfast i went up to Pewts and he and Beany sed to me gosh Plupy we broak a lot of winders in old J. Albert Clarks house and put up a sine and when i told them what they had did they were suprised as time and they sed well all rite for you old J. Albert your tirn will come. so i asted Pewts father to come down and put in a new pane of glass. and he came down before i went to school. he sed that peeple were talking about the rain of lawlissness and that sumthing was going to be did about it. he sed it probly was being did by sumone we hadent the leestest idea of, most always when sum verry unusuel crime is comitted the pirpitraiter is found to be one of the most respective citisens of the town. Pewts father sed he callated it wood be so in this case. he sed he was satisfide it wasent boys or rowdys but the last pirson we wood suspeck.

the Exeter Newsleter had a peace in it today. Beany read it to me and i cpppied it down for the record. this was what the peace in the Newsleter sed.

crime rammpent

The waive of crime that has broaken out in our comunety is one that deserves the repribation of every wirthy citisen haveing the welfair of our town at hart. the unpreceedented boldness of the miss creants is sutch as reminds one verry forceably of the why ohs of New York that infaimus band of ruffans that plunged the city of New York into a riot of criminality that bid fair to rival the orgies of Roam under the rane of Nero.

we have jest been regoiceing in the convicksion of the ring leeders of the band of garrotters that has terrorfide the naboring city of Boston when we are confrunted with a serious of crimes in our own town that bid fair to rival the wirst of the above mensioned atrosities.

the cowerdly assault upon our wirthy sittizen mister William Hobbs a man whose mennifoaled and sterling trates of carackter intitle him to a very high rank as a cittisen. the dasterdly attact up on mister Biley J. Tilton whose open handed jennorosity has done so mutch to maik his naim ornnered in this community. the repperhensibel nature of their warning to mister Isak Shute a man whose jenerous wirth and moddist life has indeered him to evryone, the coarse thret to mister J. Albert Clark whose kinliness and good deads are as well knone as his finanshal ability and probbity, are sutch as maik the blud of evry onnest man boil in their vanes.

it is indeed time that the ofisers of the law take the most astringint measures to deteck and stamp out the hoal infernal brood.

when father come hoam tonite he redd it and laffed and sed i wunder what dam fool rote that. ennyone with branes enuf to fill a thimbel had augt to know that nobudy is going to be hirt. the fellers that tide up that mud tirtles mouth aint going to hirt ennyone. the moar the fools talk about it the moar the fellers that are doing it are going to do it sum moar.

i bet old Hobbs and Ike and old Biley Tilton and J. Albert bougt 100 Exeter Newsleters apeace to send round to their friends if they have got enny.

October 25, 186—-clowdy and cold. i dident get licked today in school whitch was a releef. last nite i woak up and got thinking about the Terible 3 and what wood hapen if we got cougt and i coodent go to sleep for moar than 2 hours. i gess the peace in the Newsleters wurrid me. i wundered if i had augt to have got up the Terible 3. i had sevveral narow escaips from the reform school so father had sed and this was wirse if i got cougt. so i desided me and Pewt and Beany must be verry cairful and not leeve enny trase of our dedly wirk. bimeby i got to sleap and dident get up this morning untill mother come up and shook me. i hardly had time to get in my wood and water and eet my breckfast and hiper to school. i got there jest in time whitch was probably one reason why i dident get licked. i tell you when a feller knows his teecher is watching for a chanct to snach him balheaded he has to wauk pretty strate.

this afternoon Pewt had to help his father paint a fense and Beany went down to Ed Toles and when Beany is down there i dont go becaus it is ap to lead to trubble between me and Beany on acount of Lizzie Tole Eds sister. so when father come home early on the 2 oh clock trane he had a lait dinner and we went down to see about getting my boat up for the winter. so we rew up river to the Eddy and then rew back. we had to row hard to keep warm. well when we got back to the worf father sed less pull the old boat out and we got hold and pulled her haff way out on the worf and then father swang her round to get the stirn out and gnocked me rite into the river with my close on.

gosh it was as cold as a ice and i swum to the worf and father the pulled me out and jawed me for being a fool to get in the way when he hadent told me what he was going to do. aint that jest like him. well he made me run all the way home and then took off my close and he rubed me with a ruf towel that neerly took my hide off. it was almost as tuf as when they rubed the black off of me with bristol brick and seesand when i thougt i was always going to be a niger.

then he give me a glass of hot lemonaid and maid me go to bed. the lemonaid was all rite but i haited to go to bed. we was going to have a meating of the Terible 3 and then we was going down on the square to hear a peddler sell stuff from a wagon and a big torchlite. but father woodent let me go. but he brougt me up a new novil. it was a ripper. the naim of it is Rattlesnaik Redhead the Red Handed. we will have to have the meating of the Terible 3 tomorrow after chirch.

October 26, 186—-sunday again and raning hard. it has raned hard all day. it always ranes sunday when a feller wants to do sumthing.

none of the folks went to chirch xcept Cele who is verry religus. she is throug with the palsams and is reading the provirbs. father asted me if i gnew what a provirb was and i sed yes it was a part of speach that modifide virbs ajectives and other advirbs. then he begun to laff and they all laffed. ennyway i bet evrybody but father and mother and Aunt Sarah and Cele dident know. he sed the provirbs was the wize sayings of old king Sollerman whitch was suposed to be the wizest man in the wirld.

father sed he coodent quite beleeve that for he sed enny man whitch had as many wifes as Sollerman coodent have had horse sence or been a repsective cittisen. ennyway he sed he was wizer than old man Purington Pewts grandfather who rew out to sea 10 miles in a storm one day and when he got to the shoals where the litehouse and the big hotels was he landed and clim up the rocks and when they asted him where he come from he sed he come from America.

last nite father went to hear the peddler on the square. father got a gold stem winder wach for 2 dollers. when he got home he tride to wind it up and he cood wind it for 15 minutes and it woodent be enny nearer wound up. so father looked into it and there wasent ennything in it but the winder. so father was mad and sed if the Terible 3 wood roten eg that pedler he gessed evrybody wood be glad of it gosh i dident say nothing but you bet the Terible 3 will have a meating tomorrow erly and they is going to be sum fun tomorrow nite.

October 27, 186—-this has been a grate day for te Terible 3. this time we have did sumthing that evrybody is glad of. xcept jest a few fellers and sum wimen whitch aint willing to maik enny sackrifise for the good of the town. bimeby peeple will see that the Terible 3 is able to do sum things that the poliseman cant do.

father sed tonite after he got home that it sirved old Swane the poliseman and old Mizzery Dirgin the poliseman that throwed me out of the hall that time that father was going to make a speech but dident dass to jest rite. that it was the law that a pedler coodent pedle things without a license and old Swane and old Mizzery Dirgin knowed it and hadent augt to have aloud him to do it and if they had did their duty father woodnt have lost 2 dollers in bying a tin wach without enny wirks in it. father sed he woodent have missed it for 10 dollers and he wood like to know who done it. i sed peraps it was the Terible 3 and he sed if it is peeple had augt to forgive them for what they had did to old Biley and old Bill and old Ike and old Ward and old J. Albert. i wanted to tell him but of coarse my othe woodent alow me to tell. i bet father wood make a awful good member. if he was a member we wood have to call it the Terible 4 and then peraps Beany and Pwet wood have to have there fathers in it and we wood have to call it the Terible 6.

So i gess it is all rite to leeve it as it is, but if we ever get up another one father will have to join. jest imagine ennyone ketching us and triing to lick us when father was round.

i havent stoped laffing yet over it. if enny of the peeple whitch got pluged ever find out who done it they will kill us dead. but they wont never find it out.

well this morning i got up and et my breckfast and done my choars and went over to Beanys and got him and we went up to Pewts and had a meating of the Terible 3 and i told them what father sed and what the pedler done to hime and that the pedler was going to pedle there tonite and that it was our chanct to do good wirk and to maik a naim for ourselfs. so Pewt took us out to where his father had set a lot of hens and there was lots of hens and there was lots of egs that dident hach. sum of them was so lite that you coodent plug them verry far and sum of them whitch were heavy had ded chickings in them. we broke 1 of eech kind to see whitch smelt the wirst and we coodent tell. both smelt so bad that we had to go out of the coop and wait till it aird out. then we pluged 1 of eech kind agenst the fense. the lits one popped the loudest and the chicking one spatered the most. they was 36 left.

Well Beany sed his father was papering sum rooms in Masonick block in the 2th story for General Maston and that he was going to Portsmuth tonite to a masonick meating. so Beany sed he wood get the kee of the office and we wood go up there and lock the door and open the windows easy and not have enny lite birning and we cood see evrybody in the square and nobody cood see us and he gessed mister pedler wood think sumbody had throwed a skunk at him.

well i have forgoten wether i got licked in school today or not. i dont think i did but i aint sure. i dident think of ennything but what we was to do to the pedler and old Francis grabed me and shook me up and give me 2 or 3 bats and stood me on the platform for a hour. so i dident get licked after all. i thougt i wood remember it if i was licked.

well after supper i studded until haff past seven and Cele done all of my xamples if i wood let her read Ratlesnaik Red Head the red Handed after she had read 2 provirbs. so i let her have it and after i had coppied the xamples i hipered over to Beanys. he and Pewt were ready. we devided the egs and filled our pockets with them and then we went down town.

when we got there the pedler was standing in his wagon in the square. and he had a big torchlite and he was hollering and holding up things to sell. they was a crowd of peeple round him men and wimmen and boys and girls. we went down to masonick block and went up stairs. we dident meat ennybody and the stairs were pich dark. we unlocked the door of the office and went in and opened the winders eesy. it was lucky we did becaus Beany run into a table in the dark and broak 2 egs in his pocket. murder how they smelt. we had to stick our heads out of the window to breeth. Beany sed what am i to say to father and mother when they smell me and find i have got roten eg on my close and Pewt sed we fill say we were in the crowd and got hit and nobody will think we pluged ourselfs. i tell you Pewt is awful smart to think up things. that is why he gits so few lickings in school and me and Beany get so menny. so after we had got all the egs out of our pockets and in litle piles ready and cood breeth inside we all got ready. the old pedler had a bottle in his hand and sed now ladies and gentlemen i have here a bottel of my selibrated panyseer compounded by the most destinkwished chemists in Europe and of the purist and most xpensive drugs and warranted to cure headake, earake, backake, bellyake, hartake, rumatism, growing panes, varicose vanes, bunions, corns, ingrowing tonales, scroffuler, siattikeer, lung fevers, scarlet feever, meezles, hooping coff mumps and croop. children cry for it, old maids sy for it, you must have it. waulk up, run up, gump up, tumble up ennyway to get up only fetch your money up and all for 1 doller.

jest as he sed that Pewt let ding with a chicking eg as hard as he cood. it wood have took old mister pedler square in the head but jest then he leened down to take a doller and it went over his head and took old Mizzery Dirgin who was standing facing towerds us rite square in the mouth and spatered all over him. i bet he gumped 9 feet in the air and then begun to hoop and gag and rushed for the horse troth and put his head in and soused it round and the peeple all begun to laff and holler and old Mizzery gumped up all driping and arested Mike Prescot for being drunk and begun to drag him off and Mike held back and fit and old Swane grabed him to help old Mizzery and we let ding as fast as we cood and old Swane got one rite between the sholders and one rite in the back of his head that popped like a pistol and he let go of Mike and rushed for the troth and put his head in and while the old pedler was laffing his head off he got 2 chicking egs 1 in his shert bosum and one rite square in the eye and i never heard sutch swaring and hooping and gaging in my life and and sheriff Odlin who was standing on the curbstone got one in his stovepipe hat and of coarse he had to arest sumone and he took Bill Hartnitt and waulked him off and as soon as the old pedler got enuf of the eg out of his ey so he cood see and breeth he grabed the ranes and liked his horse round the corner. peeple were rushing round and triing to get out of the way and sum were hollering murder what a stink and sum were hollering hell what a stink and sum were laffing their heads off and bending over and slaping their gnees and leening agenst trees and holding their sides and sum were swaring and getting the polisemen to arest inosent peeple whitch hadent done nothing and one man with a streek of yellow down his back where he had got a popper was offering 500 dollers for the man whitch wood tell him who throwed them rotten egs. i see father there talking with old Swane and old Mizzery and shaking his head. father dident get hit but Pewts father did. he got a popper in the coat tale and he was mad. he wood have been madder if he had gnew it was his eg.

of coarse we hit a good many peeple that we dident meen to hit. they shoodent have been in the way and they coodent blaim ennybody but themselfs. but i supose they wood about kill us if they gnew who done it. peeple is pretty unreesonable sumtimes. but we drove the old pedler away and saved a grate del of money for the peeple and we pluged old Swane and old Mizzery Dirgin and evrybody was glad of that. of coarse when a feller gets a roten eg in the ey or in the middle of his vest when he has got his best close on he dont feel xacly plesant towerds ennybody. after tonite i gess evrybody will ware their old close when they go out to hear a pedler pedle.

well while the peeple was hollering and swaring and holding their nose and being arested for being drunk by old Swane and old Mizzery and Sheriff Odlin and being draged into the lockup me and Beany and Pewt shet the winders of the office and we come down stairs and went home. when we got to my house we all went in. mother and Aunt Sarah and Keene and Cele was setting up. well when he went in and begun to talk mother and Aunt Sarah begun to maik awful faces and Keene and Cele sed phew what a awful smell and mother sed Keene open the windows quick and sumone birn a rag. what in the wirld have you stepped in boys, go out and scrape your feet on the scraper and wipe them on the mat. you had augt to be moar cairful where you step and Beany he sed it aint that misses Shute i got hit with a roten eg when sumone roten eged the pedled and mother sed i dont want to be unpolite Elbrige, Elbrige is Beany you know, but i think you had better stand in teh doorway while you xplain. so Beany stood there and we were telling about it while Keene leened out of the window and hollered phew and mother and Aunt Sarah held their nose when father come in and the minit he come in he sed Geerusalem the golden naim ever dear to me will that smell folow me all the days of my life till i dwell in the house of the lord forever. and mother sed George i realy wish you woodent talk so befoar the children and father sed all rite Joey, he calls mother Joey you know, i wont, but it is verry triiing to a man of my partickuler disposision to return to the buzum of his familiy to find the intire homested smeling like a combineasion of a glu factory, a fertilizer factory and a ded horse whitch has been left 3 weaks in a hot July sun. and mother sed for heavens saik George dont say enny more. it is bad enuf without thinking of sutch dredful things. and father sed i wont Joey only you shood not have interrupted me and tirned me from my religious medditasions. i was doing pretty well. then Aunt Sarah sed if you aint moar choise in your langage you never will dwell in the house of the Lord but sumwhere elce, and father sed tell me sumthing new and dont scair me to deth Sarah. but how in the wirld did that smell get here, and me and Beany and Pewt all hollered Beany got a eg in the side and father sed i shood think he did and the best thing Beany can do is to go home and chainge his close. it is neerly 10 oh clock and we have got to go to bed sumtime tonite.

so Pewet and Beany went home and father set down and mother shet the winders and father told us about it and how meny got hit and what they sed and we all nearly dide laffing as we always do when father tells stories, and father sed Gim Ellison got hit in the middle of his vest and went home holding his nose up in the air so high that he run bang into a tree and broak his speckticles, and old Bradbiry Purington, Pewts father went home holding his coat tale up like a woman holds up her trane. he sed that old Mag Mackflannery got hit and went rite down to old Bill Morrils house and maid so mutch fuss that Bill promised her a new dress if she wood shet up and go home. he sed Bill sed he will never run for selickman again. it keeps him in hot water all the time. he sed Bill sed if he hadent agreed to by her a new dress she wood have drove him into a loonitick assilem.

father he sed it was wirth 25 dollers of enny mans money to see old Swane and old Dirgin get it and they hadent enny rite to arest Mike and Bill and Gimmy Josy whitch wasent doing nothing but standing round, and wasent drunk enuf to be arested, and he sed he and Amos Tuck went in and baled them all out and that was why he was lait. father sed he wished moar egs had hit the polisemen and he wished he gnew the fellers whitch throwed the egs he wood give them 5 dollars.

gosh i wanted to tell him but my othe forbid but i wish we cood get that 5 dolers. father sed if the Terible 3 done it they hadent augt to be blaimed for ennything they had done to old Biley and the others. then he told me and Keene and Cele to go to bed and we done it. while i was wrighting i remembered what father sed about baling out old Mike and Gimmy Josy and Bill Hartnitt and i hollered down stairs and sed father how did you go to wirk to bale out them fellers. and father sed i used a stomack pump of coarse. how did you supose i done it, with a dipper. now you go to bed. so i went back and shet my door.

i tell you father knows how to do things. he pumped all the rumm out of them fellers and when they are tride in coart tomorrow and old Swane and old Mizzery sware that they was drunk the jug will tell them they is dam liers and a disgraice to the perfession. i wish i cood go to coart and hear the jug say that but i supose i have got to go to school. tomorrow i will wright the report for Pewt to copy becaus i can spel so mutch beter than Pewt.

October 28, 186—-brite and fair. gosh the funniest thing happened to Pewt and to Beany. when Pewt got home his father was there and auful mad because he had got a poper on the coat tale becaus he was going to a temprunce meating tonite and was going to set on the platform and Pewts mother sed it wood be a weak befoar he cood ware that coat again becaus she wood have to boil it in 2 waters and rince it in and 3 and then dry it and ion it. so Pewts father coodent set on the platform at the temprunce meating and he was mad enuf to lick his grate granfather.

if Pewt had gnew enuf to keep still he wood have been all rite but he wanted to be funy and he sed that is a funy way to boil egs and old man Purinton grabed him and lambasted him with his ratan can till you cood have heard Pewt holler down town. it was tuf on Pewt but he dident get a lot of lickings he ougt to have got and i gess he cant complane.

and Beany had tuf luck two for when he went into the house they maid him go out and take off his jaket and his father licked him for spoling his close and maiking sutch a smell until Beany hollered as loud as Pewt. for onct in my life i had sum good luck for i got up the hoal thing and they got licked for it. i supose it aint rite for 1 of the Terible 3 to laff when the other 2 gets licked but i cant help it.

tonite we dident do nothing but put up another sine on old Ikes house it sed.

bewair Isak the hour of retrobusion is at hand.
the Terible 3

i xpect to hear sumthing from Ike tomorrow.

October 29, 186—-today neither Pewt nor Beany cood go out of the yard xcept to go to school. they boath sed they wood be willing to stay in the yard the hoal day if they cood stay away from school but

126

they thougt it was tuf to have to go to school and run the risk of being licked and then stay in the yard when the other fellers was having a good time.

but i done the best i cood to help them out. after school this morning i got a croud of fellers to go up to Pewts. they was Pop Clark and Hunny Donovan and Ham Welsh and Skinny Bruce and Jack and Gim Melvin and we staid there until Pewts father drove us out and after school this afternoon i got the saim croud to go over to Beanys so he woodent be loansum and we staid there till Beanys father drove us out. Beanys father told my father that it was more punishment for his family when he kep Beany in the yard than it was to Beany becaus evry time he kept Beany in the yard all his frends come in and rased particklar hell.

tonite old Ike sent for father and wanted to know if he wood come up and stay with him until nine oh clock when he was going to have a poliseman stay all nite to perteck him from the Terrible 3. father he sent him word that he wood be up after supper. he had to go down town a few minits and he sent me up to tell him and to say that he had better stay in and keep the doors locked. he told me to tell him he wood give 3 gnocks but not to open the doer for enyone elce.

Aunt Sarah sed George do you really think they is enny dainger. and father sed not a bit. sumone is having fun with Ike and Aunt Sarah sed why do you want to scare him to deth and father sed sister mine our gentle cussin Isak has had far two easy a life and it is a good thing to instil into his mind the idea that moths and rust do corrup and theeves braik throug and steel. then aunt Sarah tride not to laff and sed i think it is a shaim to wurry so good a man as he is and father sed.

sister thou wast mild and luvly
gentle as the summer breaz.

but it is hard to convinse you that desperrit cases need desperrit remmedies. now this is a desperrit case. verry desperrit. supose the Terible 3 shood kidnap Ike and hold him for ransum. who wood give 5 cents for Ike? who wood give ten, have i enny offers. maik it 7 1/2 cents. no offers maik it six. do i have enny offers. no by saint bride of Bothwel no let the portculis fall. and i wood have to go throug life uncheered by the companonship of Ike.

then aunt Sarah sed George do be sensible for onct in your life. jest onct. are you going to scare that poor man to deth or not? and father he sed far from it sweet sister. i shall be kindness itself. is it kindness in the docter when he conceles the faital naiture of a diseeze from a diing man and alows him to go whooping into the vast beyond without a chanct to repent. is that kindnes sister? ecco answers not by a dam site sister. it aint kindnes. it wood have been kindnes to tell him the gig was up and give him a chanct to maik his will and pay a few notes and by sum paper with black eges and 40 or 50 yards of craip for a fale for his wife.

so it will be my duty, sister, in spite of your prairs and teers, not to concele from Isak the seerius nature of the thret maid by the Terible 3. have you ever reelized how my boyhood was blited by the thrashings it received becaus i was a bit rude to my gentle cussen Ike. and do you reelize how many hundred times he was held up to me as a moddle and how i was erged sumtimes prairfuly by mother and moar often strapfuly by father to emulait his vertus. and do you think, sweet but earring sister that i will alow sutch a opertunity of asureing him of my pertecksion and simpathy to pass.

> o the demon and his bride
> and the grate grate owl
> by all his curage tride
> in the popes sanbowl

i gess not, Sarah mine. i shall go up and convinse Isak that the wicked stand in slepery plaices and that the way of the transgresor is hard. Isak has called upon his cussen for pertecksion. wood you have me fale him, speek woman.

then aunt Sarah began to laff and sed there is no use in talking to you when you are fealing like that and i shall not say enny moar and she went off. i gnew there wood be sum fun for they always is when father talks like that and so i asted father if i cood go up to Ikes with him. he sed i cood go but i must let him do the talking and not say a word unless i was asted to. so i sed i wood be cairful and we went up. it was not quite dark and when we got up there father gnocked 3 gnocks and we heard sumone say who is there, and father sed it is me George and then Ike unlocked 3 or 4 locks and opened it about 5 inchs and it was held by a chane. then he peeped out and sed is it you George. who have you got with you and father sed this is my boy Harry. then he sed to me this is cussen Isak and i sed how do you do cussen Isak and he sed how do you do and i sed i spoke to you one day and you dident know me and so i told father if he ever got a chanct to interduce me.

the Ike sed i am a little neer sited and i sed i see you are cussen Isak and then father nugged me with his elbo and i dident say enything moar.

then father sed you havent heard enything moar of the kidnapers and Ike he give a sort of gump and sed do you think cussen George that they is kidnapers and father sed i have thought so from sum things i have heard. and old Ike sed what have you heard and father sed well Isak i dont want to friten you but you had augt to know this. jist then Ikes wife Mary come in. we call her Mary Isak becaus they is so mutch alike and never goes enywhere and jest sets and rocks in rocking chairs and looks at each other.

when she come in father got up and shook hands with Mary Isak and interduced me and she asted him if he thougt they was verry daingerous men and father laffed and sed no cussen Mary there isent the leest dainger in the wirld. it is only sum smart fellers that wants to have a little fun with sum of our best cittisens and they isent the leest need of wurrying. so you go to bed and i will set up and talk with Isak until the poliseman comes up.

so Mary Isak went up stairs and Isak begun to perk up quite a lots until father sed as i was saying Isak when cussen Mary come in, i have read the papers cairfuly and there has been quite a number of cases cimmiler to this. 1 in Milton masschusetts and 1 in Lewiston maine and 2 in new york State. in eech case warnings was hung up like these and in each case a verry ritch and promminent cittisen was kidnaped and held for ransum. the man in Milton had to pay 35 hundred dollars and the man in Lewiston paid i think 48 hundred dollars they wanted 5 thousand dollars but all he cood rase was 48 hundred and the 2 in New York had to pay 9 thousand apeace. but you know prises is higher in New York. probly you woodent have to pay moar than 5 thousand.

well all this time old Ike had been setting ferst in one chair and then in another chair and puling his wiskers and when father sed this he gave a grone and sed aint there no pertection under the law? and father sed the matter is being vestigated and persecution will follow

enny falce step that the villins make. the trubble is they are verry
hard to ketch

then Ike sed isent there sum way out of it and father sed i have been
thinking Isak why dont you and J. Albert Clark and Biley Tilton and
the other fellers whitch has been warned make up a purce like you
and sum of the fellers done when they was afrade of being draffed in
the civil war to hire substitoots. then if the scoundrils get one of you
the others will help pay his ransum. well Ike he thought that mite be
a good idea and he sed he wood see sum of them tomorrow if the
Terible 3 dident get him befoar morning. then father sed dont wurry
a bit Isak while i am here they will have to get you over my ded
body and Ike sed thank you George you were always a kind frend
and father sed yes Isak we was frends but not xactly Damin and
Pithius.

well bimeby the poliseman come up and it was old Filander Kize
and he was smoaking a old black pipe that smelled wirse than one of
our poppers that we pluged at the pedler and old Ike sed have you
got to smoak that mister Kize and old Filander sed yes it is the only
thing that will keep me awake and so Ike sed well i supose i shall
have to stand it. so me and father come away after shaking hands
with old Ike and father told him to go to bed and to get a good nites
rest and not to wurry and then we come away and we cood hear him
locking all the locks and bolting all the bolts and puting up the chane
so the Terible 3 coodent kidnap him.

when we was going home father began to laff and sed i supose i was
a meen cus to wurry cussen Isak like that but all my life he has been
held up to me as a moddle and if i thougt you wood tirn out like him
i shood feal like throwing you over the brige in a bag with rocks in it.
think of living a life without fun. gosh he mite have been a useful
cittizen if he hadent been so cussed good. how ever i will go up
tomorow and chirk him up a little.

when we got home mother and Sarah was setting up and darning
stockings and Sarah sed well George did you wurry the poar man
out of his wits and father sed piece woman i treeted him with the
uttmost kindness and was a grate cumfort to him. of coarse i was
cairful not to under estimait the dainger for feer that Ike mite be bold
to rashniss and xpose himself needlessly to dainger. it wasent verry
hard to perswuade him to stay in the house for a weak or 2. indeed i
think i wood have had to fite hard to get him out. but when i left him

i asured him taht if wirst come to wirst he cood probly be able to pay his ransum if it wasent moar than 20 thousand dollers. i thougt he was going to faint ded away then and i told him with me and Melander Kize and old Swane and Mizzery Dugin and old Brown willing ot sackrifise our lifes for him he needent wurry.

then Aunt Sarah sed and she coodent talk verry well because she was triing to bite a thred off, i think i shall go up and tell cussen Isak that you are jest stirring him up and father sed he will not beleeve you for i told him the hoal family but me had tirned agenst him straingly becaus they thougt he has did sum dredfill thing that wont see the lite of day and that Harry and I are the only ones that stand up for him and Aunt Sarah bit off the thred with a snap and sed George Shute if i cood beleeve a single wird you say i shood be verry indignent, and father sed it is harroing to be so douted and missunderstood by them whitch is deer to you and he pertended to burst into teers and sed he wood go to bed and weap his piller sopping wet and he made up a auful face and winked at mother and went up stairs and Aunt Sarah sed to mother what a man he wood have been on the staige. he wood have beet comical Brown and Artimus Ward and Joshua Billings all to peaces, and mother she sed yes he wood but i prefir him jest as he is.

October 29, 186—-rany again. it hasent done enything but rane for 3 weaks. it was so rany that we coodent put up eny sines or comit eny crimes. i saw old Filander coming down from Ikes this morning and when i went to school i say Mary Isak with all the winders open airing out the house.

October 30, 186—-cold and windy. all the horse chesnuts in frunt of Sheriff Odlins place has fell down and all the fellers is stringing them on strings and pluging them over the telligraf wires. of coarse me and Beany and Pewt does it to pass away the time and devert suspishons. we have got moar serius things to think about. saw old Filander come down from Ikes again today and saw Mary Isak airing out the house again. tonite father went up again to cumfort Ike. father says that he dont think Ike cood et along without his sunny precence.

every time father comes home from Ikes he says Ike sends down town for a man to put on a new chane or a new lock on the door. father says if he goes a few moar times he will get him to put iron bars in the winders. old mother Moulton stays there days. father says he hasent had so mutch fun sence he took laffin gas and cleened out docter Johnsons ofice and throwed docter Johnson out of one winder and docter Prey out of the other and Gim Melcher down stairs.

October 31, 186—-Hork and Spit both dide today. give them a big ded rat that old mis Dire give me. they toar it into bits and et it fir and all and when i come home from school they was both ded and all curled up. i asted old mis Dire how she cougt the rat and she sed she poizened it with rat poisen only she called it rat poizen. i told her it killed my horks and she sed she was sorry but she forgot to tell me. i thougt at ferst that she done it perpose to pay me for sending her old cat to Haverhill but i gess she dident. we had a meating of the Terible 3 today and if she had done it a perpose we wood have atended to her case even if she was a woman. while the Terible 3 dont maik war on wimmen, we dont perpose to have wimmin maik war on us.

Filander is still at Ikes. tonite we drawed lots to see witch shood go up with a sine to Biley Tiltons. i got the shortest straw and had to go. Pewt had printed a sine whitch sed.

Bewaire the vengunce of the Terible 3
it spairith not the wicked man.
but it strikith in darkniss. Bewair.

when i got up there old Biley was setting by his door with a gun over
his gnees. i sed how do you do mister Tilton and he sed how do how
do. i pertended i come up to see Luke Mannix but he wasent to home
and i come back. i dident leeve the sine you bet.

November 1. J. Albert Clark has got a bull dog. he bougt it of old
Mike Casidy. he keeps it to perteck him from the Terible 3. father
thougt he had augt to have moar pertecksion and told him so. father
is verry kind to J. Albert and to Ike.

we have maid father a onery member of the Terible 3. woodent he be
surprised if he gnew it. of coarse we cant tell him he is a onery
member but he is. i asted Pewt and Beany if they dident want their
fathers to be maid onery members and they sed no, that their fathers
had licked them for nothing the nite we roten eged the pedler and
they wood voat agenst it. so that is what they get for not helping the
Terible 3.

well tonite when J. Albert come home and tride to go into the house
the bull dog grabed him by the hine leg and nearly toar his britches
off and he slamed the door on his hed before he wood let go and J.
Albert had to set in the barn while he sent down to old Mikes to get
him to come up and make the bull dog let him in. so after a while old
Mike come up and maid the dog let him in. then he maid J. Albert
feed the dog and pat him and he told the dog J. Albert was his frend
and he sed the dog gnew moar than a man and they woodent be eny
moar trubble with him after this. and he maid J. Albert pay him
anuther doller for coming up and maiking the dog mind J. Albert. it
was lucky J. Albert had on his second best close and it wasent his
best lavender britches that the dog toar. after supper tonite J. Albert
took the bull dog out for a walk hiched to him with a chane and a
coller round his neck and ferst the dog chased a cat and draged old J.
Albert about 10 rods befoar he cood stop him and the woman whitch
oaned the cat come out and told J. Albert he wasent eny gentleman
for keaping a feerosius dog and J. Albert was bowing and taiking off
his hat and asting her parden when the ferosius dog started after
another cat and J. Albert lost his hat and had to hiper a long distence
holding back with his hine legs sticking out in front and triing to
stop him and hollering whoa.

well when J. Albert got him stoped he got a stick and was going to lick him but the dog grouled and J. Albert thougt he woodent lick him after all so he went back after his hat puling the bull dog along and stoping evry time he come to a tree or a post, then he got his hat whitch had been run over by a dingle cart with a lode of hay. well J. Albert got his hat and pushed it into shaip and brushed it and put it on and started off again with the dog. and when he was going by old Si Smith store old Sis big white dog come out and piched into J. Albert dog and you had augt to have saw that fite. it was a ripper. they stood up and toar at each others gozzles and rassled and rolled over in the dirt and bit and shook and knawed each other. and old Si come out and lammed then with his cain and swoar at J. Albert and old Shep Hogden and Gimmy Bedell pulled their tales and hine legs and throwed water on them and hit them with brickbats and J. Albert pulled at the chane and hollered and Lamp Flood was a going to lick J. Albert who hadent done nothing to him when father grabed him by the neck and neerly yanked his head off and throwed him in the guter. bimeby a feller from Mager Blakes stable told Shep to pull on one dogs hine leg and Gimmy to pull on the other and when they had the dogs rite out strate the feller lit a sulfer match rite under their noses and they let go prety quick and Shep and Gimmy pulled them apart. the sulfer maid them choak and they had to let go to breeth. it was a buly fite and old J. Albert done well.

i wish you cood have saw old Lamp Flood go fluking into the guter.

November 2, 186—-sunday again. it comes round pretty often i think. Saturday dont seam to come round as often as sunday. today there was a little. this morning old J. Albert started to go down stairs and the bull dog woodent let him. i ges in the xcitement of the fite and chaising the cats he had forgot that J. Albert was his master. J. Albert gnocked on the wall and wanted father to take the kee and open the door and get the bull dog out, and father sed are you saif J. Albert where you are and J. Albert sed yes he cant get me up here but i dont want to stay here the rest of my life, and father sed if you are saif you will have to stay there till i can send down for old Mike to come up. i dont have eny grate hankering to have a bull dog hanging to me for the rest of my life eether. so maik yourself to home and reed a few chapters of the bible for this is sunday and i gess towerds supper time old Mike will come up. then J. Albert sed cant you get a gun and shoot him throug the winder and father sed it is sunday Albert and i am verry perticler about using fire arms on this sacrid day but if you will posess your sole in pashents i will see what can be did.

So J. Albert shet the window and father told me to go down and get old Mike and i done it and Mike come up with me and J. Albert throwed out the kee and old Mike opened the door and the bull dog waged his tale when he saw old Mike and wigled round jist like a puppy, he was so glad to see him, and J. Albert come down and told Mike he had ruther be kidnaped than et by a bull dog and he sed Mike had got to taik back the dog and give back his 10 dollers whitch J. Albert had gave him and Mike sed not by a dom site a bargin was a bargin and J. Albert sed he dident bargin for a dog to eet breckfast dinner and supper off of him and old Mike sed he asted for a dog that woodent let enybody into the house and he got one. and J. Albert sed he xpected to be able to get into his oan house and old Mike sed he dident say enything about that when they traded and after they had talked and jawed about it J. Albert sed Mike cood have the bull dog if he wood taik him off to onct and Mike he done it and went off smoking his old pipe and the bull dog gumped up on him and wigling his tale.

enyway aunt Clark J. Alberts mother is coming home tomorow and i wood like to see enyone kidnap J. Albert when she is around. Filander is still at Ikes.

November 3, 186—-cold as time this morning. i saw a flock of robins eeting sum red berrys on a tree. the blackberds has all gone 2 weaks ago. Potter Gorham says they follow the cost line down south stoping evry day somewhere to eet. the robins goes last and sumtimes stays here all winter. i have never saw a robin in winter but Potter sed he see one onct.

Potter knows all about birds and animals and insex and things. he is going to be a natturalist sum day. i wood ruther be a natturalist than enything in this wirld xcept a band player. so i am going to be a band player and play the e flatulent cornet becaus that is the highest and the loudest and the eesiest to carry round.

the trumboan is pretty good and if i cant play the cornet i shood like to play the trumboan. if sum feller wood maik a trumboan that wood have the 2 parts slip into eech other so far that there woodent be enything left then a feller cood put in into his vest poket when he wasent playing it and nobody wood know he had it. it wood be grate fun to taik your trumboan sliped together in your vest poket to chirch and when the old minister was preeching auful tiresum and old mister Blake and old Han. Dow and old Steve Gail and all the other men in the chirch are sleeping and injoying the sirmon verry mutch indeed thank you to taik the trumboan out of your vest poket and put it together and blow a auful toot ratetatoot as loud as you can and see all the old pods gump up and sum of them hit their heads on the phew in frunt of them where they has been leening their heads in an atitood of prair and the old minister loose his plaice and gump ten paiges to 7thly insted of 4thly. and when old C. Lovell 2th whitch is sumtimes sexton and sumtimes suprintendent of the sunday school comes round to see who blowed the horn and to put him out they aint no horn enywhere and sum folks think it may be the last trump of Gabril. if i ever get time i am going to try to maik a trumboan like that but i am so bizzy with the afairs of the Terible 3 that i cant spend eny time in sutch things as them.

Tonite we put the sine Pewt rote for old Biley Tilton on Ikes house. we had a meating of the Terible 3 and we desided that we woodent do eny moar at present to old Biley becaus when a man sets in his garden with a shot gun on his gnees and dont ast the polise to help him they aint mutch use to do enything to him. bimeby peraps we may have a chanct. we also desided not to do eny moar to J. Albert becaus he done so well in the dog fite and was so perlite to the woman when she sed he was no gentlemen when it wasent his falt becaus he coodent stop the dog from chaising her cat the ferst yank but done the best he cood. so we aint ging to bother him eny moar. so we put up a sine on his house and neerly got cougt but dident quite. it sed

J. Albert Clark. the Terible 3 has desided that they has maid a mistaik in your case. you done splended in the dog fite and you hung on to the chane and dident let go when Lamp Flood was going to lick you whitch took grate curage. The Terible 3 think you are a good feller and are your frends for life. The Terible 3.

November 4, 186—-Today Ike got old Swane to stay there. he smoaks a wirse smeling pipe than old Filander. Filander stays nites and old Swane daytimes. Ike sent for father and father advised him to have sumbody round all the time. it costs a lot of money but father says nobudy wood know the vallue of money unless they spends it. Ike thinks sumthing is going to hapen pretty soon.

November 5, 186—-rany today. i gess it was lucky it was for if it hadent been for the rane Ikes house wood have birne down. gosh the Terible 3 is fealing pretty wurried. last nite at 3 oh clock the bells begun to ring and in heard peeple hollering fire. i gumped up prety lifely and i cood hear father yelling for his britches. we got to the frunt door together and we cood see a big blaiz up towards Ikes. gosh i was scart. when father sed them devils has did it at last i thougt it was all boys play but i gess it was real. it means stait prizon for life for sombudy. i was so scart that i cood hardly maik my hine legs go but i kep up. all the bells was ringing and evrybudy was hollering fire. when we got there Pewts father and Beanys father and old Filander and old Nat Weaks and old Bill Greanleef and old printer Smith and old Parry Moulton and old Gus Brown and Pewt and Beany and evryone were pumping water into lether buckets and pales and hollering where in hell is the ingines and this is a hell of a fire dipartment and rushing round and getting in each others way and swaring and luging out the firniture and throwing crockery through the windows. old Bill Greanleaf lowered his wife out of her chamber by tying her to a sheet and then clim down hisself when all he had to do was to go down stares and out of the door. and it was only 10 feet high and they cood have gumped if necesary. old Mrs. Sawyer fainted ded away and sumbudy throwed a pale of water on her and she gumped up and called him all the naims she cood think of.

jest then the Torent No 2 come down the strete with the men on the roap running on the cleen gump. they stoped by the reservor and run out the hoze and let down the pipe and then found that they had left the nozzle at the ingine house upon the plains and they sent a feller up there on horseback and all they cood do was to pump water into pales whitch helped sum but not mutch. then the fellers formed bucket lines and kep a pumping and pouring and wondering where the Union No 1 and Fountain No 3 were.

it tirned out after the fire was over that the moon was rising in Hamton Falls and that they saw the lite and went down there as fast as they cood hiper thinking there was a big fire and when they got way up to Isiar Hanes house the moon was up so that they cood see what it was and they was so tuckered out runing a mile and a haff up hill that they coodent do a single thing but set down and sware and call each other dam fools. they was even two tuckered out to fite and most always firemen is ready to fite and so they must have been prety well used up.

well we fellers whitch was at the fire wirking our heads off and triing to save old Bill Greanleef and his wife and Ike and his wife and old Bill Morill was getting prety tuckered with pumping and hollering and throwing water on the flaims and throwing firniture throug the winders and runing ladders agenst peeples heads and saving hens by the hine legs squorking and flaping feerful and wondering where the Union No 2 and the Fountain No 3 was and what had become of the feller whitch had went for the nozzle and hadent come back when it begun to pour rane and i never gnew it to rane faster and in a few minits the fire was out. then we was going to move the thing back but we found that sum of the firemen had choped hoals in the roof of the house. the fire hadent got to the house but they thougt they wood have the hoals reddy for the Union No 1 and Fountain No 3 and the feller whitch had went for the nozzle and hadent got back when they got there. so the house was full of water and sum of the plastering had fell down on the heads of the fellers whitch were throwing things throug the winders and covered them with plaster.

well after the fire was over we went home. father says they is going to have the best detecktives in Boston to find out who the Terible 3 is. evrybuddy says they done it to get even with Ike. father says they is jest as sure to go stait prizon as he is to get his breckfast tomorow. i went to bed but dident sleap a wink i coodent eet eny breckfast this morning. mother says i must be sick. gosh it is wirse than being sick.

this morning the Terible 3 had a meating. we desided to give up the asociasion and to burn the records. it is a auful thing to have stait prizon stairing you in the face when you havent done nothing. we havent done nothing rong but if they find out who the Terible 3 is we will have to go to stait prizon. sumbuddy set fire to Ikes house sure. they wasent eny stove in the barn. if it had started in the house it mite have cougt from the chimny.

November 6, 186—- things is getting wirse evry day. i have lost the record of the Terible 3. Pewt sed he give it to me all rite but when i went to my desk it was gone. i know it was there 2 days ago. i hunted evrywhere for it. i asted mother and aunt Sarah and all of them if enyone had been in my desk and they all sed no. mother asted me what i had lost and i told her i had lost a story i had rote and she sed well you can remember it cant you and i sed yes but i dont want to wright it again. i have hunted evrywhere and so has Beany and Pewt. if enyone has found it our goos is cooked and we go to stait prizen. i have looked forward moar than oncet to going to the reform school or to jale but i never gnew what it was to xpect to go to stait prizon for sumthing you never have did. i cant eet and cant sleap. it is wirse than being ded. a grate deel wirse.

November 7, 186—-the insurance men come and xamined the fire and took measurements. they desided it wasent Ikes falt or Bills falt and so they pade them. father sed Ike and Bill maid moar money than they had for six months. but he sed that the insurance companies was going to find out who done it and it looked to him that the Terible 3 would be looking throug bars before long. i cant hardly breeth when i think of it. i saw Beany and Pewt today and they are so scart that they cant eet or sleap just like me. of coarse we have got to laff and holler at fellers and play football but we only laff to concele a braking hart. i wood give a milion dollers to know what has become of them records. if i had birnt them we wood have had sum chanct. and if we had the sence to put sum other fellers naims in it peraps we mite escaip but i dont see enny hope.

November 8, 186—-brite and fair. i wish i felt as good as the wether. it seams as if evrybody was looking at me and saying he done it. he is 1 of the Terible 3. evrytime i see a strainge man i think he is a detecktive and evrytime i see old Swane or old Mizzery or old Filander or old Brown i wunder if they is going to grab me and put the handcufs on my rists and drag me to the lockup. mother says she is going to see docter Perry about me but i laff and say i am all rite. peraps she wood tirn from me with lothing like Dolly Bidwell done in East Linn when she plaid it in the town hall last winter, if she gnew. jest think less than a year ago i was going to shows and having a good time and now i am wateing to be sent to stait prizen. i have often wundered how fellers felt whitch have to go to stait prizen but now i know.

November 9, 186—-sunday again. it mite as well be sunday as eny other day. perhaps they woodent arest a feller on sunday. Beany had the docter today. i asted Lucy Watson what was the matter with him and she sed Docter Perry sed he was in a low nervus stait. she sed Docter Perry sed if Beany had eny mind he shood say sumthing was praying on it. the minister preeched on the wicked whitch fleas when no man persuith. that wood be all rite but detecktives is pursuing us. i wish he hadent sed enything about it. i wish i cood be let alone in chirch.

November 10, 186—-Pewt had the docter today. he had docter Swet. docter Swet thinks Pewt is thretened with brane feever. father says that cant be. he sed he shood as soon xpect me to have brane feever as Pewt. i think peraps we will all feal better when it is over. what i am afrade of is that Pewt and Beany may go crasy and say i done it all. what if they shood. i wood give a milion dollers if i gnew where them records have went to.

November 11, 186—-Beany aint eny better. i went over today to see him and see what cood be did and he sed he dident want to see enybudy. i went up to see Pewt and asted old man Purinton how he was and he sed he was getting no better verry fast. i wunder if he has heard enything.

November 12, 186—-Pewt aint enny better. Beany aint et ennything but broth for 2 days. i still eet to keep up my strenth. i am wurried about them. if they get two week peraps they will comfes and say i done it. i hoap they is man enuf to keep their othes. i am going to keep mine.

i forgot to say wether it was brite or fair or rainy or enything fer a weak. i dont remember and i dont cair a dam. there i have sed it.

November 13, 186—-father keeps looking at me quear. i wunder if he suspecks ennything. if i had only told him he was a onery member peraps i cood tell him about things without braking my othe. i bet he wood help us. we have got to have sum help. it wont do to let Pewt and Beany dy and leeve me to go to stait prizon alone. if 1 of has got to go to stait prizon the hoal 3 of us has got to go. Beany and Pewt aint going to sneek out of it by dying. that woodent be fair.

November 14, 186—-i have gave up haop and dont cair now. i am only wateing till a poliseman grabs me. i got licked in school. it dident even hirt me. it maid me think of sumthing elce but stait prizon for a few minits. old Francis says i am getting nummer evry day. he says if i dont waik up he will have to waik me.

what is the use enyway. last Sunday the minister sed evrybudy cood get the gratest cumfort from the bible whatever his truble was. he sed open the bible and reed the first virse you see and it will comfort you. so today i saw Celes bible open where she had left it. she is reeding Isiar. i dident know eny part of the bible was rote by Isiar. Isiar Hanes was probably naimed after him, well i thougt i wood do as the minster sed. so i shet up the bible and then opened it and the ferst virse i saw was this.

by these 3 was the third part of men
killed, by the fire and by the smoak

it was in chapter 9 virse 18 of Revellasions. you cood have gnocked me down with a fether. i shet up the book and set down. then i got out the dicksionery and looked up Revellasions and it sed

revellasions—-the ack of disclosing to others
that whitch was ungnew to them.

so what is the use. i wish i was ded.

November 15, 186—-the gratest thing has happened. i feel as if i cood fli to the moon. jest think i am in my room wateing for father to come and lick me and i aint wurrid a bit. i have et haff a mince pye and i never taisted enything so good in my life befoar. i feel so good that i wood like to holler. jest think i aint got to go to stait prizon nor Beany nor Pewt. this morning Pewt and Beany were faleing verry fast and the last i heard of them they was setting up in their shirt tales eeting meet and potatoes and pye and evrything.

well tonite father went out and mother asted him where he was going and he sed low so i woodent hear him up to Brads. i heard him and i thougt sumthing was up. so after he had went out i folowed on and saw him go into the paint shop. Pewts father and Beanys father and General Mastin were there. so i crep up where there was a broaken winder and lissened. father set down and took out of his poket, what do you think, the records of the Terible 3. i was so sirprized that i neerly hollered but dident. then father sed well gentlemen i have the infirnalist record of yuthfull depravity i ever read in my life. and then he read it and evry time he stoped to breeth old General Mastin wood slap his gnee and holler god did you ever hear the like of that, the little devils. and father wood holler and laff and Pewts father and Beanys father wood two. then father wood read sum moar and then he sed i wish i had been a member and i almost sed you was an onery member but i gnew enuf not to.

bimeby he finished and sed there General did you ever hear enything like that in your life and General sed he never did. then father sed he suspecked us from the ferst and peraps he was as mutch to blaim as we was becaus he stirred up old Ike and J. Albert but when the fire come he was wurrid as the devil althoug he felt sure we hadent done it he was afrade sum dam fool wood try to lay it onto us. and the very day of the fire he found the records where i had droped them. he told Pewts father and Beanys father and they thougt it woodent hirt us to wurry and they told the 2 docters and the docters sed they was all rite and it woodent hirt them.

then father sed it was only fair that he and Pewts father and Beanys father shood pay for eny damige we had did. and Pewts father sed as long as i got it up father had augt to pay. and father sed why do you say that and Pewts father sed becaus he always does get the other boys into truble and father kind of smiled and handed the records to him and sed whose writing is that.

and Pewts father looked at it and sed hum haw and that was all he cood say. Father dident know that i rote them becaus i cood spel so mutch better than Pewt and Pewt coppid them.

then General Mastin sed Ike and Bill has maid money by the fire and these little devils dident have enything to do with that and that it cougt from hot ashes enyway. now i am counsil for the boys and i aint obliged to tell a thing about them or who they are. a lawyer aint obliged to. i will put a peace in the paper saying enyone whitch has sustaned eny damige from the so called Terible 3 can by proving there damige under othe to me will be pade. and you may be sure that they aint a man living that will be willing to sine the kind of a staitment i will draw up for him, and General laffed and they all did two.

then father asted General what his bill was and General sed hell the only thing he wished was that he cood have been a member of the Terible 3 and if father wood give him that record to keep to look at when things was going rong to cheer him up he wood call it square. so father give them to him. then i started to creap away and i cougt my foot and come down with a bang and in a moment father come out on the cleen gump and grabed me. then he sed well sir what have you been doing lissening and i sed yes sir and he sed you start yourself for home and after Clarence and Elbrige, they is Pewt and Beany you know, have had there supper i will come hoam and atend to your case. so i come home and i am wateing for him to come and lick me and i dont cair. enybody whitch cant stand a licking when he knows he has escaiped stait prizon aint mutch of a feller. gosh aint it good to feel good.

November 16, 186—-brite and fair. father dident lick me. it is fun to be alive.

November 17, 186—-Beany and Pewt has got well again and has come to school today. we have been wundering if a onery member had eny rite to give them records to enybudy. of coarse we dont cair but we have been wundering.

November 18, 186—-brite and fair.

THE END

Lightning Source UK Ltd.
Milton Keynes UK
UKHW010733170621
385673UK00001B/54

9 781006 857812